RISK AND RICHES

AVA FOX

CONTENTS

PART I

CHAPTER ONE: JAMIE

Who is this girl? There's something about her that intrigues me, that has piqued my interest far more than anyone else I've met in a while. I feel strangely drawn to her. I want to get to know her more, but I know that's a bad idea with everything that's going on. My father is trying to put me in a single category, drive me mad with new business ventures as he criticizes me every step of the way. My mother, on the other hand, wants no part in my father's financial playground, but instead, she's furthering her own dreams of gardens, book clubs, and people striving to be her. I'm tired of this fake, snobbish world. I just want to feel something other than the quick fix of a pleasurable night out or the alcohol running through my blood. I want my life to mean something more.

I sat at my desk in my office, perched at the very top of the high-rise building owned by my father. This was his territory, his preferred stomping ground, where he made every last financial decision that could make or break the future of the company. For such a long time, I didn't care if the hedge fund came crumbling down, and I didn't care if one risk meant the end of the line for our financial gain. I just wanted to find the next beautiful receptionist to sleep with. My priorities were different now, and they had been for a very long time. I wanted to feel something that wasn't rooted in talk of wealth, fancy parties, or what was on the menu for dessert after a long night at the office.

I couldn't help but let my mind wander off to what it was like sitting across from Audrey, a fresh-faced writer who Cece, my unrelentingly egotistical ex-girlfriend, hired to cover the story about her perfect life. Cece was the kind of woman that always wanted the best, and when she found herself bored or unhappy with her current circumstances, nothing ever stood in her way when she sought out something better. That was the case for our relationship, and I'd never been able to forget that she had done the one thing I never thought she'd do—sleep with my best friend.

It wasn't something I liked to think about, but seeing Cece sitting there right next to Audrey, a girl who had no idea what she was getting herself into, made me long for an escape from my world. I was tired of the overdramatized version of my life, and I wanted to indulge in something that felt somewhat normal again. There was nothing about my life that was remotely normal, but that didn't matter. What mattered was that I continue finding ways not to go insane on a daily basis. I had been craving an escape for a while, and it was one of the reasons I ended up slipping into an old, lumpy sweater, throwing on a ball cap, and heading out to the part of town where no one would think to pay any attention to me.

I had stopped in at a little local bookstore that had gotten quite a bit of press for being known as a local landmark for how long it had been standing, and that was where I first laid eyes on Audrey. Her blushing cheeks and vibrant smile were enough to draw me in, but I didn't think I had any place talking to her. I let her get back to her job, but there was a part of me that wished I would've at least said hello. I know she caught sight of me before I took off, and she must be wondering who I was and what I was doing in her little bookstore. The way she saw me the day Cece had invited her to chat a bit about her upcoming position wasn't the way I wanted her to remember me. I wasn't sure why I even cared so much about this stranger's opinion of me, but I didn't want Audrey's perception to follow what everyone else had been thinking for years—that I was a washed-up Princeton graduate who has had a silver spoon in his mouth from the time he could walk.

If I knew Cece, the only reason she had me meet Audrey was to gauge whether I was remotely interested in or flirty with the woman and writer who was going to be following Cece around to get the inside scoop on her life. I wasn't in the mood to play her games, so I gave her the nod of approval, leaving her to feel like she was well on her way to winning me back even though I knew that was never going to happen. I didn't have it in me to forgive Cece for what she did, and I didn't think there would ever come a time where I'd find myself changing my mind.

I ran through a few of my emails, replying to anything urgent, and called in for my assistant to grab another cup of coffee for me to get through the rest of the day. With all the time I spend here, it would seem like this is where all the drama in my life would come from. Not the case, I thought, reminding myself that my mother was throwing yet another dinner, where I'd have to be present, suited up, and ready to mingle. I'd much rather be holed up in my suite, pretending like I had no pressing responsibilities. I didn't want to deal with having her jump down my throat about not being there for my family. Even though I didn't care much about what they planned to do on an everyday basis, showing my face was going to go over a lot better than ignoring her persistent invitation.

Returning to my parent's house was never something I liked to do because it reminded me of how much of a mess I was when I was younger. I got into far too much trouble for a teenager and left my parents to clean up my messes. I always wondered if that was why they were so hard on me these days, but even then, they should've started to back off the moment I decided it was time to move out. I was successful enough to do just fine on my own, but my father insisted that I join him and continue to be a part of his world. I was reluctant at first, but he promised to open up the kind of doors for me that would let me go off on my own whenever I chose, but that never happened. Every time I brought it up, he'd shoot me down like we never had that conversation. It was his way of saying that I should be grateful for what I had and to stop going after what he thought I wasn't ready to achieve.

Not a day went by where he didn't ridicule me for my performance in the office, a deal I made, or a party I attended. A lot of my lashing out in my early twenties was because I wanted to openly defy him, but since I'd gotten older, I'd learned that was simply a colossal waste of time. My new mission was to beat him at his own game and garner the kind of reputation that would overshadow him for a change, and that meant that I had to play with the sharks. I had to go off and do the things that would make him absolutely furious, step into the limelight on my own, and start making a name for myself that didn't have the weight of my family's legacy.

The Forrest name in this country signified wealth, and my father liked to refer to himself as a self-made man even though he was born into his riches like the rest of his friends. I wanted to show him what it would be like to break away from the crowd and do things differently, but that meant I would have to defy him differently. No more parties and sneaking women into the house. No, it was time to start going after the business ventures that would make it clear I wanted out from under his precious empire.

My day was already quite glum, but once it was time to head home for the day, I got pulled aside by my assistant, and she had a pretty concerned look on her face.

"What is it, Victoria?" I asked, watching her smooth the ends of her pleated skirt, eyeing the door to my father's office.

"I don't know if I should be sharing this information with you, but the boss just went in with a few of the board members. I don't know what they're discussing, but he's chosen to keep you out of the loop. I just thought you should know," said Victoria, keeping her voice low while she pretended to finish up some work.

"Thank you for telling me, Victoria. It's no wonder Mother has asked me to come by a bit early," I said, and she nodded, acknowledging that I didn't want to be questioned any further about what was going on.

I was already quite tired of my father going behind my back to make decisions without me despite that I was just as vital to the success of his business as he was. I decided that if there was ever a time to start ruffling his feathers, it was right then. I set my briefcase down on Victoria's desk, straightened my tie, and sauntered over to his office doors. I turned back to see Victoria go white as a ghost, and I mouthed, "It's okay," to let her know that her name wouldn't be thrown around in all of this.

This is between you and me, Father.

"Well, what is going on here? I must've missed the memo," I said, swinging the door open to see them all sitting there, staring back at me blankly.

"Jamie, yes. This isn't a matter that concerns you at the moment. I think you should be getting home. Your mother is going to be expecting you," my father said.

I took the seat at the far end of the table right in front of him, shooting him an arrogant smile, watching him trying to keep calm. "I think I'll stay. If I'm not mistaken, I believe that Mother is expecting both of us back home, isn't that right?"

My father gulped, readjusting the papers in front of him while he reluctantly continued the conversation. He kept glaring at me, letting me know with that single expression that he was going to deal with me later when we were finally alone. It was exactly the move that made my night, though, reminding me that I was starting to step out of my shell, and sooner or later, I'd be able to make the shift away from his business to my own.

THE BLACK town CAR PULLED UP to my PAREnt's driveway, and I glanced up at the beautiful home with the large stone columns and perfectly trimmed shrubbery lining the property. I hadn't been back in a very long time because my mother rarely ever kept her dinner parties at home anymore. I was surprised to learn that she was even bothering to have everyone over, but I knew her well enough to know she was trying to impress someone. I was on a roll, and I wanted nothing more than to figure out who she was trying to kiss up to. I entered the large foyer, glancing around at the crowd of people clinking their glasses together under the soft glimmer of the chandelier overhead.

It felt strange to be back, to have all the crazy memories begin to flood back, and it was quite nice to see how far I'd come in such a short amount of time. I looked around, trying to find my mother. I made my way into the kitchen because I had an inkling she was back there, probably yelling at the catering staff yet again. It seemed to be her favorite hobby because it was the only thing in her life that she could control.

"Hello, Mother," I said, seeing her over by the sink, clutching her pearls. Her hair was tied up in a perfect French twist, and she looked back at me rather disappointedly from under her faux perfection.

"Jamie, I'm so glad you're here. Has your father come with you?" she asked, and I could see the hope behind her eyes that he was already here, even if he had not bothered to say hello to her before mingling with the guests.

"No, he hasn't arrived yet. Do you know that he had a little meeting with the board members, which he chose not to include me in? I made sure to check in with him before I left, even catching a little piece of his plan to tear down a few of the city's oldest hotels to put up condominiums in their place. It's not the kind of discussion that would be had at a hedge fund, now was it, Mother? Did he hold that meeting at the office thinking that I would've come here?" I asked, knowing quite well that my mother was a terrible liar, and the look in her eyes told me everything I needed to know.

"He's trying to look out for you, Jamie. He doesn't want you involved in anything that could damage your reputation, especially if it goes south. He wants to keep you on the forefront, running his business the way he intended you to all this time. Aren't you happy, Jamie? What more could you possibly want?" she asked, shooting the kitchen staff and waiters a fake smile whenever they were in earshot, telling them they were listening in on a private conversation.

"I want to know why Father refuses to give me any real responsibility. I've done everything he's asked, and he still treats me like I've just turned twenty. Like I'm out drinking every night and pretending to ignore all of my duties. That isn't who I am anymore, Mother. I haven't been that way for a very long time, and I'm not sure why you and Father can't see that," I said, feeling the frustration begin to well up inside me.

"He's worried that you're on a short fuse, Jamie. It wouldn't be the first time that you promised to upkeep your father's reputation and turned around to do something that would damage it. He's looking out for himself, and when he thinks you're ready, he will be sure to give you the responsibility you so desperately seek," she said firmly, reaching in to caress my cheek and pretending that she had any maternal instincts at all.

I quickly removed her hand, letting her know that I didn't want her sympathy, not about this. She was in no position to side with my father on the fact that I wasn't ready to accept more responsibility. I wanted to tell her right then that she should think twice about who she spends her life defending, but I decided against it. Instead, I wanted to let her know what I had in store for my father.

"You and Father have no idea what I'm capable of, and when the time comes, you're going to wish these conversations went differently. The only thing you both have ever cared about is keeping a united front. Well, I may decide that I don't want that anymore. I may decide to stray away from your precious little family and go off to do something on my own. If you and father truly think that I'm not ready to handle what's out there for me, then it's probably time I prove you both wrong," I said, getting the last word in.

She looked shocked. I'd never talked back to her, not when I was sober, level headed, and very clear in my thoughts. She was one to always write off anything I said out of anger, but this time, I was quite sure I'd struck a nerve. She didn't even bother to yell at her staff or go back out to the crowd to mingle with everyone. She made a move for the back staircase, heading upstairs to blow off some steam before the first course.

I knew I had pissed off a lot of people, and I was probably going to have to pay for that once the dinner party was over, but I didn't care. I was on a roll, finally telling my mother and father how I truly felt. I wasn't going to let them dictate every move I made for the rest of my life, and I wanted to make sure that they were well aware that I could pick up and leave at any moment. If I let them continue to control me, it would be only a matter of time before I'd dug myself so far into their empire that there would be no way for me to break out, stray away, and make a name for myself. The time to start making moves was now, and I believed I knew where I could start.

The one thing my father lacked was his communication with society, and his pull started to dwindle because the world believed he was invincible. He was shielded by his wealth his entire life, and he never had a connection with the world around him. He operated on a socialite schedule for someone that prided himself on being a businessman. I planned to show him just how much of a mistake he'd truly made.

Sorry to say, Father, there are better ways to go about running that precious business of yours. When I finally have one of my own, I'll be sure to clue you in.

CHAPTER TWO: AUDREY

had my laptop nestled on the pillow on my lap, trying to get a bit of writing done. I was reaching over for my lukewarm cup of tea when I heard my cell phone ring. I took one look at the number, realized who it was, and wondered why she'd be calling so late.

"Hello, Cece?"

"Audrey! I'm so glad that you're still up! Listen, I know you have to be at work tomorrow, and I promised not to uproot your whole schedule, but something has come up, and I need it to be included in the overall story. I'm going to be shooting for an up and coming designer first thing tomorrow, and I need you to capture the entire experience. I hope that won't be a problem," she said. I had only spent two days following her around and trying to get a feel for her life so that I could write the story about her, and I was already growing rather tired of it.

"I don't know, Cece. I promised Henry I'd be at work for the entire day tomorrow," I said, trying to plead with her. I already knew what she was going to say, so I braced for her telling me that I needed to take my position a bit more seriously.

"You want your name in the byline, right? That was the deal. Your first published story. This is a requirement, and I know your lovely boss will understand. See you tomorrow, and if all goes well, I might just drag you to this party I'm attending tomorrow evening," she said, like taking me to one of her snobbish parties was going to make up for the fact that I was abandoning half of my responsibilities.

"Of course, Cece. I will see you tomorrow," I said, and she hung up the phone, leaving me to deal with abandoning Henry another day at the bookstore.

I was secretly hoping that Cece's life would start to get boring so that I could head back to Greer's and at least pretend I was going to stick around for a while. I wouldn't be surprised if Henry fired me, though. He had every right to at this point. The truth was, my job at the bookstore was my only source of income. Even with a promise of getting my story published in Coeur, I still wasn't sure if I was getting paid. Cece hadn't specified payment, and I now believed that she was preying on my want to be published since she hadn't mentioned anything about paying me for my work. I should've known better and brought it up earlier, but maybe it wasn't too late to ask.

I heard rustling coming from Claire's bedroom while she sauntered out groggily, making her way over to the kitchen for a glass of water. She wasn't the least bit surprised to see me awake, and I could already tell that she was trying to wake up enough to ask me what was wrong.

"You look terrible," she said with a light, tired chuckle.

"So do you."

"What did your socialite snob say now?" she asked, realizing that I wasn't enjoying much of the high-profile lifestyle.

"She wants me to come to take notes and capture the

scene while she gets her photo taken in these new designer clothes. What's new? She's been driving me crazy, but I'm doing what I can to keep it together. This really could be my big break," I explained, and Claire nodded.

"I know how bad you want this, Audrey. I just don't want to see you get hurt in all of this. You come home exhausted every night, you're barely at work, and I'm worried about you."

"It's going to be okay. It can't be much longer until Cece's mother is going to need a copy of this story on her desk, and then I can go back to my normal life of trying to figure out how to get my writing out there on my own. I need this to get my foot in the door. You know that," I said, and she smiled encouragingly.

"Well, you know I'm always here if you need to talk. I can't imagine that it must be easy to bottle up all the dirt you get on these people every day. It must be so interesting to step into their world for a little while," she said, filling her glass and trotting off back to her room.

"Trust me, you don't even know the half of it."

I shut my laptop, dragging myself to bed, knowing that I had to be up early to get to Greer's before opening so I could beg Henry not to fire me again. He'd been such a sweetheart about the whole ordeal, telling me to follow my dreams and that there'd always be a spot open for me if things ever got more hectic. I knew it wouldn't be long before he decided to hire someone else in my place, and I had to be prepared for that to happen. I had no other way of earning any money, though. I had just gotten the job, and I hated being torn between trying to make a living and following my dreams. If this opportunity hadn't come when it had, I might never have put my writing out there. I had to remember that this wasn't going to be easy, but eventually, it was all going to pay off. I slipped under my duvet, trying not to worry about potentially losing my job or my chance to make it as a writer.

THE NEXT MORNING, I stoppED IN AT GREER's to HAVE another uncomfortable conversation with Henry about how I was going to miss work again. I could tell from the look on his face that he was starting to get fed up with my absences. I glanced down at my wristwatch on the way out, realizing that I had to make it to the shoot within the next fifteen minutes. Otherwise, Cece was going to kill me. I ran to catch a cab, knowing there was no way I'd be able to make it on foot, but when I finally hailed one down, someone got into it from the other side.

"Oh, no you don't!" I screamed as I opened the door, slipping inside to beg whoever was in there to let me ride with him. He looked up at me from under his ball cap, and I was shocked to see who was sitting next to me. "Jamie? This is the last place I would've expected to see you."

He only stared back at me like I'd just uncovered his terrible secret. "Audrey. I take it you need to be somewhere," he said, keeping his answers very short.

"Unfortunately, I do. Do you mind if I share this cab with you?" I asked, wondering why he was even in a cab at all.

"Of course," he said and asked for my location so he could tell the driver where to drop me off.

I didn't know what to say to him, nor did I know why he wasn't suited up in the back of his shiny town car, heading to the office like I imagined. He was dressed down comfortably, and he looked so normal. I waited to see if he was going to bring it up in conversation because I didn't want to be the one to pry into his personal life. It frankly wasn't any of my business, but I couldn't help but be a little curious.

"I hate to ask, but should I leave out meeting you here when I see Cecilia today?" I asked, and he nodded politely.

"I don't want her to know what I'm up to. I'd appreciate it if you kept this between us," he said, and I smiled.

"What are you doing around these parts, anyway?"

"I needed to get away from my hectic schedule, crazy parents, and crazy ex-girlfriend. Please, do not tell Cece I said that, either. Along with everyone else, she has gotten on my last nerve," he said, and I could tell that he was genuinely upset.

"I'm sorry to hear that. You don't have to worry. I won't mention a thing," I replied. "You know, I saw you at the bookstore a couple of days ago. I was about to ask if you needed any help, but you took off. I recognized you when Cece invited me to that meeting, but I didn't want to say anything. It was night and day, though, and I didn't want to pry any further. It really isn't even my place to be asking questions right now."

"No, no. It's all right, Audrey. I know that this may come as a shock to you, especially after spending time with Cece and knowing where I come from. The truth is, I've been tired of that life for such a long time now, and I've been trying to figure out a way to find my purpose again. For such a long time, it was just about spending money, throwing lavish parties, and not caring about the consequences, but now things are different. Now, I want to have a genuine conversation with someone who isn't going to try to rope me into something," he said, and I could see his expression shift, glancing out the window so he wouldn't have to meet my eyes while he told me how frustrated he was.

"If you ever need to have a genuine conversation, I can promise I won't try to rope you into anything," I said, just trying to be nice, but he looked back at me like I was speaking an entirely different language.

"I'd really appreciate that, Audrey. Thank you. You know, I really did mean what I said about liking your story. It was a fresh perspective on what it must be like to move into New York with a dream, and trust me, I've seen many people come here to do that. It was nice to see that there are still genuine people left in this world," Jamie said, smiling.

"I appreciate that. I honestly didn't think that I would hear back from Cece or anyone from Coeur when I sent that submission in. I hardly remember sending it in at all, but it's landed me here now, and it's a chance to make a name for myself as a writer. That's all I've ever wanted," I said, and I realized it felt nice to get all of this off of my chest.

"I think you have what it takes to go very far, Audrey. The only thing I will tell you is not to let any of these opportunities overshadow what you're truly good at. I know that Cece has enticed you with the whole idea of having your name in the byline of a magazine for your first published story, but there's more to writing than that. When that story finally goes to press, I can get you in touch with one of my buddies who works in publishing. Then, you can have a real conversation about your future," he said, and I couldn't believe the words coming out of his mouth.

"You don't have to do that, Jamie. That's incredibly kind of you."

"Please, it would be my pleasure," he replied.

CHAPTER THREE: JAMIE

I didn't think that I would run into her again like this. I never thought that I'd allow myself to divulge my inner thoughts like that, either, but something about Audrey made me feel like I could trust her. I'd be lying if I said it wasn't refreshing to talk to someone that wasn't heavily involved in my world, and I even found myself wanting to do it again. With her being so close to Cece right now, I was afraid that it was going to cause too much unnecessary drama for me to be around her, but I couldn't seem to help myself. I wanted to see her again.

I rummaged through my closet, looking for something casual yet appropriate to wear to the little get-together a friend of mine was having at his home that evening. I had a feeling that Cece was going to make an appearance because we were all friends once, and something told me that she might bring Audrey along to capture her perfect little outing. I could already tell by the look on Audrey's face in the cab that she was done with Cece's games and tired of the way she was being treated, and she hadn't even fully written the story yet. That was the way of Cece. She promised you the world until she got what she wanted from you, and it was usually all downhill from there.

I glanced out the window, taking in the soft haze of the sunset streaming in through the balcony doors in my room. I had opted for working at home for the past few days because I still hadn't worked out things with my father. Frankly, I was at my tipping point, and I really didn't want to see him until I had enough insight into where I was headed. I was tossing around a few ideas, trying to figure out some new business ventures of my own, something that would put my name on the map without the shadow of my father's businesses following me around.

I looked over towards the other corner of my room, noticing the old typewriter sitting there, untouched and ready to be used again. I thought about it for a moment, wondering what it would be like to write a book, meld my two worlds together, and give back some of the knowledge I'd gained over the years. Father would truly hate that, but that was probably the reason I thought about giving it a shot. I walked over to the typewriter, brushing my fingers over the cold, worn keys. I wondered if I was fit to be giving financial advice to the general public or if anyone would even care to hear what I had to say. If there was one person that could shine some light on doing hefty research and turning out a piece that authentically felt like me, it was Audrey. That would give me something to break the ice with to have a conversation where neither of us felt hounded by our surroundings.

It was the perfect way to get to know Audrey a bit better. I wanted her to feel as comfortable talking to me as I felt when talking with her. She had a sense of calm about her, one that made me feel instantly connected to her in a way I hadn't with anyone else in such a long time. I wanted to feel like that again, and this upcoming party was the perfect way to steal her away for a little while to pick her brain. I felt my cell phone buzz in my pocket, and I answered it while I continued filtering through clothing options.

"Are you ready for tonight?"

"I think I may be, Will. You said that this is a small get-together, right? Not too many people, and not too many unfamiliar faces?" I asked my friend.

"You know how these things go, Jamie. I can't predict what's going to happen, but right now, that's what it's looking like. Trust me, I know you need a break from all those frustratingly perfect dinner parties your mother has been throwing lately. We're going to get a little drunk, be a little reckless, and forget about the world for tonight," said Will, and while that sounded like a theoretically good idea, I had to let him know that I wasn't going to let myself go again.

"As long as I don't end up on the cover of another tabloid magazine, I can consider the night a win. Hey, I meant to ask, would it be all right with you if I brought a buddy of mine along?" I asked, thinking of someone who might be able to help me with my idea.

"Bring whoever you want, man. My home is your home," he said, and I could hear someone shouting at him in the background.

"Is that your mother again?" I asked, chuckling.

"Actually, it's my girlfriend, but sometimes she makes me feel like I'm still living with my mother."

"Give my best to Liz," I said, hanging up the phone.

I sighed, deciding on a deep blue dress shirt and complementary tie. I ran my fingers through my hair before heading out for the evening. I could only imagine the things that were going to happen under Will's roof. That was usually the place where all the crazy parties started. We were a bunch of rich kids trying to break the elitist rules, and that made our parents incredibly angry. Sometimes, I allowed myself to remember what it was like to be that reckless and carefree, but even if I had the chance, I didn't think I would return to that kind of lifestyle.

I wanted to branch out and show my parents that I was finally in charge of my own life. My first step in doing that was to make sure I was getting my name out there in a way that didn't involve my father's businesses or my drunken debauchery. I dialed the number at the bottom of my contact list to invite an old friend to Will's house. I was sure he'd be willing to help me out with my master plan, and I was almost sure that there would be someone else in attendance tonight that would love to meet him.

I HAD my CHAUFFEUR DRop ME off AT WILL's HOUSE. I remembered what it was like when I was younger, escaping away from my parents for the night to indulge in a little bad behavior. Some things really don't change. I ascended the stairs with an expensive bottle of whiskey in my hand, and then I rang the doorbell and waited for someone to answer. The door swung open to reveal Liz, with her perfectly tousled blonde hair and piercing blue eyes, lighting up the minute she saw me.

"Oh my God, Jamie! I'm so glad that you were able to make it. Will has been driving me mad trying to get everything to be perfect, and he thinks I'm the one acting like his mother," she said.

"You heard that, huh?" I asked, laughing.

"I hear everything. Oh! Is that for me?"

"It's all yours," I said, handing over the bottle while she beamed. We walked over to the liquor cabinet in the entryway to store it with the other expensive bottles that weren't to be touched this evening.

"Make yourself at home like you always do, Jamie. Have a drink, mingle, and remember we're leaving work at the door," she said, and I nodded.

If only it were that easy, Liz, I thought, heading over to the bar Liz had set up for the evening. I ordered a drink from the bartender while I kept my eye glued to the front door. I really hoped Audrey was coming tonight, but I had to remember there was a chance that she might not show up, though I knew how disappointed I was going to be if that were the case. I wanted to have another lovely conversation with her if I could get her away from Cece without Cece getting the slightest bit suspicious. I had to try.

Right before I downed the last of my drink, I saw Cece saunter in. She smoothed her tight champagne-colored dress and tossed her coat to one of the wait staff without even saying a word. I worried for a moment that she may have come without Audrey, but just as I was about to give up hope, I saw her walk in behind Cece. Her hair was slick and pulled back behind her ears, her black dress hugged her curves perfectly, and she was propped up on what appeared to be a rather expensive pair of heels. It seemed that Cece had gotten to her wardrobe.

I looked over in her direction, waiting for her to see me. I didn't want Cece to catch onto us locking eyes, though. Finally, Audrey nodded at me, acknowledging my presence, and I saw Cece pull her away. Audrey reluctantly pulled out a little brown notebook to pretend to write down this exquisite evening. I was surprised that Cece would so readily bring her to a place like this, especially because it wasn't the kind of thing that Cece would want to be captured in her feature story. I had a feeling that she had a plan for Audrey that neither one of us was aware of.

Cece was always one step ahead of us all, and if I wanted to make sure she wasn't planning on bringing any harm to Audrey, I had to get inside her head. I had a strange feeling in my gut that told me Cece wasn't going to give Audrey all that she dreamed of, and it wouldn't be the first time she used someone innocent to get what she wanted, ignoring all of the promises she made in the beginning. If that were the case, I wasn't going to stand for it or let her get away with it, but I still had to learn Cece's intentions. It was probably a good idea to corner Cece first, get a feel for what she has Audrey doing here tonight, and then figure out how to get a moment with Audrey alone. I saw them split ways while Cece went around kissing everyone lightly on the cheek, exclaiming how wonderful it was to see them all.

Once Cece's eyes locked on me, her toned legs strutted over to where I stood. She tilted her head to read the expression on my face, as though she was gearing up to get under my skin again.

"I was hoping I'd see you here," she said, grinning at me.

"I had a feeling you'd be here, too, Cece. I see you brought your writer with you. I thought Liz said that we were leaving work at the door tonight. Unless you didn't get that memo," I said.

"This isn't about work, Jamie. I offered for Audrey to accompany me tonight as a reward for how wonderful of a job she's doing. She's been gathering a lot of great information on me, getting the perfect outline of my perfect life for my feature story. Isn't that wonderful?" she asked with a familiar devious look on her face.

"You offered an invitation to one of our private parties because she's doing a good job? That doesn't sound like the Cece I know," I replied.

"Well, if you must know, she's been looking a little down lately. I've been working her really hard, and while I'm going to be heading to the Hamptons tomorrow morning, I thought I'd bring her along for one last lovely evening before she goes back to that drab bookstore she works in until I return. Hopefully, she'll find someone here to talk to. She's been rather uptight. She probably needs to let loose, don't you think?" she asked, and it was like music to my ears to hear that she was going to be out of town for a few days. This really might be the chance I was looking for to get to know Audrey.

"I'm sure you're all the company she needs," I said dismissively while I tried to find Audrey in the crowd.

Where are you, Audrey? I think it's time we have another chat.

CHAPTER FOUR: AUDREY

W hy had I let Cece convince me to come to this thing? I didn't know anyone, and I was completely out of my element. She said she wanted me to continue capturing her life, and if I wanted to do that, then I'd have to live it a little. Yet, I couldn't help how incredibly uncomfortable I felt. She told me that she was going to be out of town on a last-minute trip for a few days, and honestly, I couldn't wait for the break. I wanted to return to work and feel somewhat normal again.

I couldn't have imagined how overwhelming this entire situation would be, and now I couldn't wait to get away from it all. This was probably exactly how Jamie felt every day. I remembered how he looked at me the minute I walked in the door. I worried that he probably thought I looked out of place and like I certainly didn't belong, and he'd be right. I wasn't sure why I cared so much about what he thought of me, but I couldn't help but think about the conversation we had in the back of the taxi.

He had felt like a completely different person there, and I

was starting to think that my perceptions of him had been terribly wrong. I wasn't sure if I was going to get the chance to talk to him like that again since Cece was breathing down my neck every few minutes. Though I hoped she'd get preoccupied talking to someone long enough for me to get a few more words in.

She went off with the woman who I assumed was hosting the party due to how stressed she looked and how she immediately jumped into complaining without even bothering to acknowledge my presence. I didn't mind. I felt better being invisible as opposed to everyone gawking at me because I didn't belong. I took a deep breath, making my way over to the table with the hor d'oeuvres perfectly laid out on fine china, reaching for something to eat. As I ate, I felt a light tap on my shoulder.

"Hello, Audrey," Jamie said, and his voice was warm like honey, much different from how I remembered it before.

"Jamie, it's nice to see you," I said, turning around to meet his gaze. I noticed there was something different about him, but I couldn't quite put my finger on it.

"You look absolutely stunning," he said, and his words sounded genuine, but I couldn't believe him with the way I felt.

"You think so? I feel incredibly out of place and like I'm in way over my head. This technically wasn't a work obligation, and I don't think I'm going to get much material for the story. I'm not sure why I bothered to show up," I said.

"I'm quite glad you did because there is someone arriving very soon that I'd like you to meet," he said.

"Who is that?"

"His name is Preston Autry. Does that name mean anything to you?" he asked, smiling back at me.

"Preston Autry? As in the co-owner of the Autry

Publishing Company? Are you sure that's a good idea, Jamie? My writing is nowhere near ready for something like that. Even talking to him, I'm not sure I'll be able to keep my sentences straight," I said, overwhelmed at the very idea of speaking to someone in publishing, let alone someone who had that big of a reputation.

"Nonsense. Your writing is incredible, and it's time you start looking into other opportunities since this story you're writing for Cece won't last forever. I wanted to give you some other options, maybe a book even," he said, and I couldn't believe the words that left his lips.

"You can't be serious."

"I am very serious, and when you two are done having a chat, there's something I want to talk to you about. I know Cece will be out of town tomorrow, and she did tell me that you were going to be heading back to work, so would it be all right if I pop in during your break?" he asked, and I wondered what was so secret that he couldn't tell me right then.

"Of course. Is there a reason we can't discuss it now?" I asked.

"It's not something I want to get out, especially since I'm not sure if it's something I want to do. I don't want anyone overhearing the conversation. Trust me, it's book-related," he said, and I nodded at him.

"Do let me know whatever I can do to help. You've done so much by getting me this connection with Preston, and you really didn't have to do that, Jamie. It's very kind of you," I said, truly believing that out of everyone I'd met in this world, Jamie was one of the good ones.

"I think your writing deserves bigger audiences, Audrey. That is the truth," he said.

I never thought of my work that way before. It was something I'd always dreamed of but never thought I'd get the chance to pursue. "I don't know how to thank you," I replied.

"Don't thank me yet," he said with a playful wink.

There was something about the way he looked at me that made me blush, and I couldn't help but feel butterflies rise in my stomach whenever I was around him. I felt like a teenager again, trying to navigate all these foreign feelings that hadn't come up in a very long time. I had to get out of my head, though, especially if I was going to have to impress Preston Autry whenever he did make his appearance.

"Will you introduce me to Preston?" I asked him.

"It would be my pleasure."

My heart fluttered inside my chest at the idea of what meeting Preston Autry would be like, but when the time finally came for me to share a few words with him, I worried that I was going to fall short. He was the kind of person that many people tried to make a good impression on in the past, and I wouldn't be surprised if he thought I was just as dull as everyone else he's met with the dream of becoming a writer. I put my drink down, watching Jamie and Preston approach me while they both dawned a smile.

"Preston, I'd like you to meet Audrey Harlow. This woman has an excellent way with words, and I think you two are going to have quite the time discussing some of the stories she's written," Jamie said, and Preston grinned at me warmly, which was rather unexpected given how notable he was in society.

"It's nice to meet you, Audrey Harlow. Jamie tells me that you have a few stories under your belt and that you're working on the piece for his incessant ex-girlfriend. It's such a shame that she got to you before I did because I would've been able to give you much more of an opportunity if your work does live up to what Jamie has said. Though it's not too late, and when you're finished with that article about New York's most annoying socialite, feel free to give me a call. We can discuss something a bit more exciting." he offered, handing me a card that was neatly tucked away in his suit pocket.

"Thank you very much, Mr. Autry. This is quite a dream come true," I said, realizing that I was probably oversharing just how excited I was. I couldn't help myself, though. I'd been looking for an opportunity like this since I moved to New York, and I couldn't thank Jamie enough for being the one to give it to me.

"Please, dear, call me Preston. Don't thank me yet. There are a lot of people in line for a publishing deal, and the only way I'm going to be able to see it through is if your work is good enough. Send me a few pieces once you've wrapped up the article for Cecilia, and we'll go from there," he said, and I nodded.

My heart was bursting with excitement, and I was absolutely beaming while Jamie came up to me to offer congratulations for hitting it off with Preston. I was so afraid that I was going to put my foot in my mouth and blow the entire opportunity before Preston even had the chance to speak, but I was glad I was able to keep it together.

"You made quite the impression on him, Audrey. I have to say, I look forward to seeing what kind of incredible work you two are going to do together," he said, grinning at me.

"It's all thanks to you," I said, grateful for how much he'd done for me in such a short amount of time.

"If you really want to pay me back, say you'll have dinner with me once Cece is out of town and you finally get a moment alone to yourself," he said.

I was a bit taken aback by his request, and I wondered

why he would want to have dinner with someone like me. "I don't know if that's such a good idea, Jamie. Cece seems like she has eyes and ears everywhere, and the last thing I want to do right now is upset her," I said even though I was secretly hoping I'd still muster up the courage to take him up on his offer.

"She doesn't have to find out, Audrey. Please?" he asked, playfully pouting while I chuckled.

"Such a charmer. All right, but only after she's gone and settled into the Hamptons. I still have work down at the bookstore, but I can certainly slip away for an evening," I said, and he beamed.

"It's a date."

Is it? I still can't believe that someone like him would even be remotely interested in me. I also have to think about what it's going to be like if Cece ever catches wind of this. I know how much she wants to keep her claws in Jamie, even if he does seem like he wants nothing to do with her. I'm worried that I'm only going to get hurt if I'm not careful, but I have to see this through. I know I'm only going to regret it if I don't take Jamie up on his offer now. He's been nothing but kind to me, and I can't help but notice just how attracted I am to him. This may be the most dangerous thing I can get myself into, but I don't think I'll be able to stay away.

I headed upstairs to use the bathroom, which one of the wait staff pointed me to, but once the door swung open, I saw Cece there with her tongue in some man's throat. I covered my eyes, turning away so that she didn't think I was staring. The man pushed past me, heading out of the bathroom while she started after him.

"Eric, wait!" she screamed, realizing that she wouldn't be able to keep up with him. She turned to me, glaring at me with such anger in her eyes for the honest mistake I made.

"You didn't see anything here, got it? Don't you dare breathe a word of this to anyone," she warned.

"I didn't see anything," I said.

Her tense shoulders softened, and she flipped her hair to the side before heading back down to the party, wiping the smudged lipstick from around her lips.

Who was that?

CHAPTER FIVE: JAMIE

started to feel an incredible weight lifted off of my shoulders. I felt like I woke up to an entirely new world of possibilities now that Cece was out of town. I couldn't remember the last time I had time alone where she wasn't tracking me down trying to get me to help with her schemes, even though I made it painstakingly clear that I wanted nothing to do with her after the way she hurt me. I knew the only reason I bothered to entertain her games was because she would not stop until she got the answers out of me she wanted. Now it was finally time for me to start focusing on my own life, though. I couldn't wait to visit Audrey and see what she had been up to. I wanted to have a conversation with her without the worry that someone would be looking over our shoulders every minute. It dawned on me that Cece had people in her inner circle who I assumed she told to keep an eye on me, as she always did, but I didn't care.

The only reason I didn't get involved with Audrey was because I didn't want to jeopardize the opportunity she had, and I knew that if I were to come between the two of them,

Cece would make her life a living hell. I wasn't sure Audrey was ready to deal with something like that, but I was starting to think that she was strong enough to handle it. Audrey didn't seem fazed by Cece, even though Cece was doing everything she could to push her around. I promised myself that I wasn't going to poke and pry too much into what Audrey's plans were after the story finally broke, but I knew that I wouldn't be able to help myself if I got the chance.

After seeing how well Audrey hit it off with Preston Autry, I realized I had the perfect opening to spend more time with her while she gave me a little advice on what it was really like to write a book. I was an avid reader, but I didn't know the first thing about getting my thoughts down on paper. I felt so free whenever I was with her, and I had a feeling that she was going to be the key to helping me write the book that was going to kickstart my move from underneath my father's shadow to a career of my own. My parents were hounding me, trying to get me to focus on whatever trouble they had brewing. Even after I made it incredibly clear that I was planning to move away from their lavish lifestyle, they always found a way to rope me back in, even if it was just long enough for me to make an appearance. My life was chock-full of elegant parties, frustratingly boring functions, and just about everything else I hated about being born into money.

I still remembered a time when it was all I ever wanted, when I didn't care how much my parents pushed me around because I enjoyed being able to do whatever I wanted. Now I was starting to see through their outer appearances to who they really were behind closed doors. The last thing I wanted was to turn out like them—to not care about anything else apart from making sure everyone in my inner circle knew how much money I made and how much power I had. It wasn't going to stop them from trying to get me back on track, especially since I could tell that they started to feel like they were losing me for good. At this rate, they were probably right.

I straightened my tie and ran my fingers through my hair while I finished up the bit of work I had left for the day, hoping I wasn't going to run into my father on the way out of the office. He still had yet to have my head for crashing the meeting where he was negotiating a deal that I should've had every part of. He may have told my mother that he was only keeping me out of it because he was sure I wasn't ready, but the truth was, there was a part of him that was afraid that I'd surpass him. He feared I would one day take over the company and do a better job than he ever could. His empire stretched beyond that of his hedge fund, and I knew he wasn't going to give any of it up without a fight, which was why I had to take my options elsewhere.

I wanted the world to know who I was—who I truly was —because only then would I be able to reach an audience that he never could. It would start with a book, but with all the knowledge I'd picked up over the years, it was truly going to be the beginning of something extraordinary. I just had to make sure that I didn't let anything get in the way or sabotage my dream. I knew quite well how easy it would be for someone to steal this opportunity right from under me, especially if I were caught in the wrong place at the wrong time.

The only piece of advice I ever heeded from my father was that no matter how successful you manage to become, there would always be someone out there waiting to destroy you. Sharing the knowledge that he taught me with the public was certainly going to put a dent in our relationship, but I didn't care because it was time someone showed him what it was like to have a little competition. He was so sure that no one was ever going to take a chance on me while knowing what my last name was and where I came from, but

I was determined to show him and everyone else that doubted me that I was capable of so much more than they realized.

I knew my way around the market. I knew how to play the field, take risks, and invest in the right decisions. Yet, I always got caught up in petty drama that stood in my way. Whether it was problems at home, my mother going off on a drinking bender, my father sleeping around, or my ex-girl-friend cheating on me, something always took my mind off what was important, and I was tired of being held back.

I was starting to distance myself from them all as much as I could, but there was the off-chance my mother would make some ridiculous demands, telling me that I had to show up and be a part of the family or else she and my father were both going to make sure I had an incredibly hard time. I had to keep up appearances where I could because the last thing I wanted was any of them catching wind of what I was up to. I may have hinted to my mother that I wanted to break away from the family business, but I knew she'd never take me seriously until I made the first real move.

I headed home that evening to change, getting into something a bit more comfortable before I went to pick up Audrey. As I got ready, I eyed the typewriter on my desk as if it was calling my name. I wanted to do more than just give the world the kind of business advice that would be the reason behind an influx of startup companies and ambitious creators. I wanted to give them an inside look into what my life was really like. The one thing my family had to hide behind was that no one would dare spill any truth about what went on behind the scenes for the fear of having to deal with the consequences, but I was starting to see that I didn't have that fear anymore. The more time I spent away from them, the more I began to see that they never had my best interest at heart, and every decision they made regarding me was to further their own agendas.

It was time the world got to see them both for who they really were, but I knew that if I wanted to write about the truth, I was going to have to position myself right in the middle of it all even though I wanted to step away for good. I wanted to continue distancing myself to show them that I no longer cared about what they did and who they stepped on to get ahead, but I might have to get closer to them if I wanted the world to see what they have been hiding.

I thought about it for a moment, and just like that, the idea began to consume me. I found myself tapping away at the old keys with the ink coating my fingers until I glanced down at my wristwatch and realized if I didn't leave right then, I was going to be late. I felt rather strange heading back into the heart of the city to meet someone because it was always where I went to escape, but now I had something to look forward to that I was never going to have back home.

Once I arrived outside the bookstore, I saw Audrey with her hair pulled back in a low ponytail, her eyes glimmering under the streetlamp lighting while she blew away the wispy pieces of hair that framed her face. She was turning the sign to say the shop was closed, and our eyes met right at that moment. I watched her face light up when she looked back at me, putting her finger up to let me know that she'd be just a minute. When she finally came out, I felt an incredible wave of relief wash over me. We finally had the moment alone that we'd been looking for ever since we were sure Cece had left town.

"You made it. There was a part of me that thought you weren't going to show," she said teasingly.

"How was I going to miss our first real outing now that you're that much closer to being let out of Cece's grasp?"

"It has felt strange to be back here, getting back to my

life, especially after seeing what her life is like. It makes me think that I'm missing out on more than I realized," Audrey said, and I could see the sliver of sadness in her eyes like she truly believed that she wanted more. She seemed tired of how her life was currently.

"Trust me, everything that you've seen and written about over the last few weeks is all for show. The truth behind what the people in my world do to get where they are would scare anyone away, and that's how they manage to keep their circles so small," I said, watching her furrow her brow.

"If it's all so bad, then why stay?" she asked, turning the key in the door to lock it before we headed off walking down the sidewalk.

"I suppose it's because as much as I want to say I'm ready to leave everything about my life behind, I just can't seem to part with it—my family, my career, everything that has supposedly made me who I am. I've grown tired of it all over the years, and I haven't been given the chance to figure out what I want," I confessed, and I watched as she listened attentively, hanging onto every last word.

"Well, I see that you're beginning to figure that out. Otherwise, we wouldn't be here right now. I thought about declining your offer, especially because Cece would kill me if she knew I was here with you, or anywhere near you for that matter, but you did ask for my help with something," she started, and I realized I hadn't had the chance to elaborate further.

"For a very long time, I've been living in my father's shadow, going by his rules no matter how terrible I felt about them. I watched him take advantage of people and use people to get to where he is today, and I didn't want to be a part of that anymore. I didn't want to feel like that was all my life was destined to be, so I made the decision to do something to give the world an inside look into how things actually operate around here," I said, and she nodded.

"You're planning on exposing your family's secrets, and here I thought you were going to be writing a book to guide people on how to start building businesses," she said, and I was surprised she was able to read me so well.

"Let's just say I'm looking to do a little bit of both. Though, I have to ask you, Audrey, please do not tell anyone what my plans are. If one word slips about this, I'm going to be shunned away from the community before I have the chance to get enough on them to start writing," I said.

She placed a comforting hand on my shoulder, letting me know that she wasn't going to breathe a word about this to anyone. "You want to make waves, and there's absolutely nothing wrong with that. If I had half the guts you did, I would've already been working on a book for Preston Autry, but I'm scared that he's not going to be as receptive to my new material," she said with a grateful smile.

"I want to show the world what my family is really like and the decisions they've made to get them to where they are. I want to share advice with an audience that trusts me, and in order to gain that trust, I'm going to have to show them the truth about what they've been speculating on for years. I can tell that my father and mother are both up to something, but I can't figure out what it is. They're both trying to keep me out of a few business deals, but I have yet to find out why that is," I said.

"Could it be that they're just trying to do what's best for you? I'm sorry, I know that's a stupid question," Audrey said.

"Not at all, but I see you still have to learn about what it's like where I come from. I know that you've spent some time with Cece, capturing her life on paper, but you have no idea the lengths people like my father would go to in order to make a few extra millions," I said, and she looked shocked to hear me say that.

"I wrote an exposé on Cece that she fully dictated, and here you are about to break away from your birthright with a book that's going to cause a social and economic storm. I have to say, I'm in full support," she said.

I turned to her, stopping her in her tracks so I could get a good look at her expression. I wanted to know what she was really thinking and how she truly felt about me wanting to do the one thing that would change my life forever, but the look in her eyes was genuine.

"Are you? You know this is going to come with an entirely new disaster once the news breaks, right?"

"I think it's brave that you want to do this, to make a name for yourself the right way without having to hide behind a security blanket of wealth and fear the way your parents do," she said, and I couldn't be more grateful that she was being this honest with me.

"So, you don't think I'm crazy?" I asked.

"Maybe just a little bit, but you are the man that helped me get in touch with one of the biggest publishing companies in the country, and I have yet to pay you back for that. So, whatever I can do to help you write this incredible, groundbreaking book about the New York elite and all the suspicious business practices that come along with it, you can certainly count me in," Audrey said, and I could tell the look in her eyes was one of determination as well as gratitude.

"I don't know the first thing about writing a book, but I'm sure that you do. I'm sure that once this is all over, we're going to be sharing incredible stories about what it's like on the other side of this," I said.

"Unlike you, I have nothing to write about, but I can certainly give you a few pointers on getting started. When it comes to finding something to write about to impress

Preston Autry, I'm going to have to dig a little deeper," she said, and I noticed the soft glimmer in her eyes that told me she was starting to figure it out.

"Well, if you're up for a wild ride on exposing one of the richest families in New York City, I'm sure it's going to change your life enough to find something to write about. That is, if you're up for it," I said.

"I'll tell the world my story if there's one to be told, but right now, let's focus on helping you," she replied, tapping my shoulder playfully while we continued our walk down to a local restaurant.

It amazed me how different we were, yet how wonderful it felt to be there with her. She gave me a fresh perspective on life that I never had before, and I was not sure I knew what to do with that information. She and I shared a similar dream that led to entirely different goals, and I could only hope that wouldn't cause complications for us later on. I wanted to expose my family's practices to the world, but I didn't want Audrey to get wrapped up in something she couldn't handle. I wondered what her take on all of this was going to be and what she was going to bring to Preston Autry when this was all over. I would have to wait and see.

CHAPTER SIX: AUDREY

I sat across from a man I once believed would never give me the time of day, and here I was discussing his plans to expose his family through writing a book that would shake the country. Everyone knew enough about the Forrest family to see how much power they had, but I wondered why he'd chosen to rope me into all of this. Did he call this a date just so I'd agree to help him? Did he introduce me to Preston Autry just so I could give him enough to get started? I wanted to believe that his intentions were pure, but I had to make sure that I didn't let all of this get in the middle of my dreams. He didn't know the first thing about writing, and if I was going to help him succeed, I would have to make sure there was something in this for me, too. I remembered everything I'd learned from watching Cece out in her own little world. I couldn't be too careful when it came to helping the people that made me start to think differently about the New York elite.

I could tell that Jamie saw my expression fall. I tried to focus on his words, but I couldn't help suddenly feeling like I was being used. I didn't want to act like I knew where his head was at or why he really asked me out to dinner. I knew that I was starting to feel something for him. It was right then that I began to question whether helping would be the best thing for me in the long run because while he had somewhere to run when things got bad, I certainly didn't. I had to do what I could to look out for myself as well.

"What's the matter, Audrey? Was it something I said?" he asked, pouring me another glass of wine.

"You've been nothing but nice to me since I took the job for Cece, Jamie, but I have to ask you something, and I want you to answer me honestly."

"Of course," he said.

"Did you just bring me here tonight because I could help you write the book that's going to kickstart your career?" I asked, gulping.

"Is that what you think? I asked you here because I think you're an incredible woman. You share a perspective about my world that no one else seems to see. Frankly, I asked you to dinner because I like you, and anything I said about the book had nothing to do with that. Even if I wasn't planning on using that book as a scapegoat to get me out from under my family's reign, I still would've asked you out," he said, and his words comforted me. They made me feel better because the last thing I wanted was to be betrayed by the one person that let me in.

"Oh, I'm sorry. It's just with everything you said about the book, and you introducing me to Preston Autry, I was worried that was all you wanted me here for," I said truthfully, but he shook his head.

"Whatever my plans are, Audrey, I'm never going to come between you and your dreams. I know that you have big dreams, and this book is just a way to establish myself in society, but it isn't something that's going to consume my entire life. I asked you for help because I wanted an excuse to get closer to you and get to know you, but I know I've done a terrible job at that because all I've done is talk about myself," he said, realizing that he'd been so consumed with his family problems that it had started to overshadow every other part of his life.

"Jamie, I meant what I said. I think you're brave for wanting to do this, and I still have yet to thank you for everything you've done for me, I just wanted to make sure that I wasn't getting in the middle of something I had no business being a part of. If you truly want my help, though, I will be there for you," I said with a smile.

"I'm sorry if I put a damper on our evening with all my talk about destroying my family image. I promise to be on much better behavior next time I ask you out," he said, smiling.

"Oh, there will be a next time, will there?" I asked, poking fun at him.

"I'm sure hoping there will."

I GOT HOME THAT EVEnInG AND FELt A RATHER unfamiliar weight in the pit of my stomach. I threw my purse onto the couch, noticing that the house had been quiet since I left. I knocked on Claire's door to see if she was sleeping. She was out cold yet again, and I headed into my room to change, sit down at my desk, and work on finishing the final story I prepared for Cece. She gave me firm instructions that she wanted the first draft completed by the time she returned.

I was just happy to get it finished because now I had

much more to think about than looking for a new job opportunity. I had been speaking to a man that was trying to undo the terrible things his parents had done to get him to where he is and show the world there was much more there than what everyone on the outside could see. I knew this would be his opportunity to start fresh, break away from his family's hold, and finally become his own person. He was playing a dangerous game, though, because in exposing his family, he was going to make it difficult for those at the top to want to trust him again.

I sat there for a while, editing Cece's story and trying not to think about all the bad things that could happen to Jamie if the book didn't turn out the way he wanted or if the story itself was stripped from his hands before he got the chance to share his side. I knew he was adamant about being truthful. For a moment, I had thought that the only reason he was trying to get close to me was so that I could help, but the fact that he openly admitted to liking me and wanting to spend time with me made me much more confused than anything else that happened tonight. It got me thinking about my own career and about what kind of stories I wanted to tell, and I realized I'd spent so much time trying to figure out my place in the world that I hadn't really gone out and done anything worth writing about.

I was now interested in a man that was forced into a finance career from the time he was eligible, forced to keep up appearances around his wealthy family, and forced to present a united front to the public when that was never how Jamie wanted to claw his way to the top. I could only imagine that he had exceptional advice to give and a lot to say about the world he'd been brought up in, but I was scared that if the word got out about what his plans were, there would be too many people standing in his way, keeping him from succeeding. I dwelled on the memories of everything I'd experienced since I agreed to take the position to write the story on Cece's life, which would be plastered on the shiny pages of her mother's magazine so that the world could continue to be jealous of everything Cece had. The more time I spent in that world, the less I wanted to be a part of it, but I couldn't help but be intrigued by it all.

The only thing that felt genuine about it was Jamie, and I knew that if his plans were to ever go south, he would have no one but me by his side, rooting for him. I wondered if that was why he clung to me as hard as he did and why he asked for my advice when he could've been having meetings with his connections in publishing. I truly believed that he cared about my opinion. He wanted to see what every other normal person out there saw, and I gave him that insight, but I could only hope that it wouldn't get us into any trouble. As much as I wanted to help Jamie, I was afraid that by getting involved, I would be the one to blame for someone getting to him before he could break his story. As long as this stayed a secret between us, I truly did not have anything to worry about. Though, do any secrets go untold in that world?

There were so many people I had yet to understand, those who I'd seen in passing when I was following Cece around, trying to get a good look into her everyday life. There were those who would do anything to get her attention and those who couldn't wait to talk about her behind her back when she was out of the room. I wondered if she had always been that way or if the lavish lifestyle, the wealth, and the fame changed her. Writing that story about her life only made me realize how shallow it was, and there was a part of me that genuinely felt worried that the closer I got and the more I pretended to be a part of that world, the more it would consume me.

Jamie Forrest was writing a book that would break him onto the scene as his own businessman. He was doing things differently from his father and being open to sharing his knowledge with the world without sugar-coating the ugly, but I realized that I didn't have that kind of drive or ambition begging me to write. I was searching for a story that would be worthy of being published by Preston Autry himself, something that would make everyone second guess what they thought they knew, and I had a feeling that I was going to find it by taking the first ticket directly into the heart of Jamie's elitist world.

In a world of socialites and secrets, there was bound to be a story somewhere, something that would pique everyone's interest. Though, I had to be careful. I knew that by writing about those people, it would only add me to their list of enemies. If Jamie planned on being on that list, too, then we had much more in common than I initially thought. I was starting to think that there was room for us to join forces, tackle both sides of this lifestyle, and tell the public what they deserved to know.

"HEY, AUDREY. WAKE UP!" CLAIRE SAID, SHAKING ME awake. I'd fallen asleep at my desk yet again.

"Oh, no. Am I late again?" I asked, sleepily.

"No, you're fine. You have about two hours before you have to be out the door, but I decided to wake you a little earlier so you can have something to eat and so we can catch up. I feel like I haven't seen you in forever," she said, and the truth was, she hadn't.

Ever since I'd been working on Cece's story, I'd been so busy that I didn't even have much time to think. Ever since Cece took off to the Hamptons, I was wrapped up in Jamie, and I didn't even know what a break felt like anymore.

"A lot has been going on lately, and unfortunately, I don't

think I'm allowed to talk about any of it. Though there is something I can share. Jamie introduced me to Preston Autry of Autry Publishing, and Preston asked that I send him some pieces, which I did, and he did like them. I'm looking for something to write about that he's going to find interesting, something that's going to do well on the market right now, and it's the first time that I believe I have a possible story," I said while we both headed into the small kitchen. I stuffed two slices of bread into the toaster while I started the kettle for some tea.

"That's incredible! Jamie has been really nice to you, hasn't he?" she asked, and I could tell that there was a bit of apprehension in her voice.

"Yes, he has. Why? Is something wrong with that?" I asked her.

"No, but don't you find it strange that you two barely know each other, and now you're spending all this time together, and he's introducing you to people that can further your career without wanting anything in return?"

"That's what nice people do, Claire. I asked him point-blank why he'd been inviting me out so much and doing such nice things for me, but he genuinely said it was because he likes me. I don't know what to believe at this point, but it's the first time in a long time that I'm genuinely happy, and I'd appreciate a little support," I said, pouting while I stuffed the toast into my mouth.

"I'm all for supporting you, Audrey. You know that. I just worry that you're going to get wrapped up in Jamie's world, and you're going to forget why you came to New York in the first place—to be a writer. You want to tell your own stories on your own terms, and I don't want anything standing between you and your dreams," Claire said, and I appreciated that she was looking out for me.

"Thank you, Claire. I've been trying to find something

life-changing to write about since I moved to New York, and when I'm with Jamie, I truly feel like I'm closer to that. There's so much that I can learn about being in his world, and while he has his own agenda when it comes to what he wants to achieve out of life, he promised not to stand in the way of mine," I said, but she didn't look convinced.

"As long as you're being careful. Men like him are quick to tell you that they don't care about what their families think until they're put in a situation where their families are all they have. Whatever Jamie is trying to do, I need you to be careful because the last thing I want is for you to get thrown under the bus," Claire said.

"What makes you such an expert?" I asked defensively.

"I see them a lot at work, Audrey. They think they can break away, turn their backs on their families, and create lives of their own. Then, they fail, and they have nothing left but resentment. I've seen it happen to too many high-profile lawyers, and I'm only telling you all of this because I don't want him to hurt you. If you truly believe that his intentions are good, then I will try my best to do the same, but a little doubt isn't going to hurt," she replied.

"I'll be careful," was all I could say because I didn't even want to give the possibility any thought.

I didn't think that Jamie's world could get any more dangerous than it already was, and I barely scratched the surface of the drama he was dealing with. I began to think about what Claire said, and I was starting to think that maybe she was right. Maybe this was Jamie's way of lashing out because he wasn't living the life he wanted, but I wouldn't be able to be sure of that unless I spent more time with him.

No matter what, I couldn't ignore everything he'd done for me and all he'd done to reassure me that he wants to move on with his life. Though, maybe having a little doubt could keep me grounded through all of this, especially if it did go terribly wrong. Maybe there was a part of Jamie that felt like once this book was out on the market, he would not have any use for me anymore, even after he told me it wasn't like that. I just had to be careful. I had to make sure I didn't let anyone walk all over me.

CHAPTER SEVEN: JAMIE

I t had been a few days since I first took Audrey out to dinner, and ever since then, I could see her start to feel withdrawn. Something had been bothering her. She had been nothing but nice to me, even if she had appeared distracted, telling me everything I needed to know to properly start writing. She gave me advice on how to give the advice I needed to write out and how to speak from a personal level so people would want to hear what I had to say. It was going to be a big moment for me when this book finally hit the shelves because every little piece of advice my father had given me over the years was going to hit the public, along with the truth about how he did business. It was time that someone challenged him and time someone knocked him off the pedestal that he had no place being on, but I was beginning to worry that all of this was consuming me much more than I liked.

I'd been writing for days, and it was finally time to meet with Preston to talk about the current progress and whether the material was good enough to be published. I wanted to bring Audrey along with me, but she told me she had to work, and I respected that even though I couldn't understand why she was so quick to leave. I worried that I'd shared too much with her or that maybe she was starting to look at me differently now that she saw the truth about my world and how terrible it could really be. I couldn't blame her, but I didn't want this to come between us. I didn't want to lose her, and I had to find a way to convince her that everything was going to be all right.

I told myself that I would give it the day, have my meeting with Preston, and show up to surprise her later that evening when she got off work. I glanced down at my wrist-watch, heading downstairs to get into the town car I had brought around for me, but I bumped into someone on the way out. I looked up to see a face I hadn't seen in a very long time, one that made me immediately angry. I was ready for a fight, and it was barely nine o'clock in the morning.

"What are you doing here? I thought I made myself clear when I told you to stay away from me," I said, and he stared back at me, smirking at me like he didn't care about my threats anymore.

"I thought about it, and to be quite honest, I almost let you run me out of town, but that was until I heard about something that made me come crawling back. I've heard talk of you stirring up trouble for your family, Jamie. You've been acting out, and I'm here to tell you that behavior has to stop," he said, and I was trying to keep myself from punching him straight in the jaw in front of all these people.

"How could you possibly have heard about any of that, Eric?" I asked him.

"You see, Cece isn't too good at keeping secrets, and she tends to keep tabs on you no matter where she is. I'm surprised you haven't picked up on that by now, Jamie. I'm here to tell you that whatever stupid plan you're brewing, it needs to stop. I can't have you ruining things for me," Eric said, and I couldn't believe that he had the audacity to say such things to me.

"You mean like you ruined my relationship with Cece? She slept with you when we were still trying to figure things out, and you were supposed to be my best friend. I have nothing else to say to you, Eric, and I'm certainly not going to stand here and listen to your demands," I spat.

"That's a shame, Jamie. I suppose I'll see you at your family dinner tomorrow evening. My family will be in attendance, too, as will Cece. I suggest you find yourself a date because the last thing you need is to show up at your parents' house without one. You know how your mother gets about putting on a show," he said.

I gritted my teeth, realizing that the dinner had completely slipped my mind. I remembered when I had been debating not going at all, but now I knew that was no longer an option. If I was going to be giving good advice and exposing the ways of people like Eric and people like my father, I had to be front and center at that dinner tomorrow night.

"Goodbye, Eric."

I walked away and got into my car, trying to shake just how angry his presence made me. He was the last person I expected to see, and I was starting to think that acting out against my parents had been a mistake because I could already feel that something terrible had been in the works. I couldn't let whatever it was deter me from my goal and getting this book out to the public so everyone could finally keep their mouths shut and allow me to live my life.

I clutched the briefcase in my lap, trying to calm myself down as my chauffeur drove me down to the Autry Publishing building, where I was supposed to sit with Preston to go over my next steps. I felt better about having sworn him to secrecy because this was certainly not the kind of thing he'd ever put his name on, but I drove a hard bargain. I gave him an opportunity he couldn't refuse, and it was only a matter of time before we were one step closer to having it hit the shelves.

Once I pulled up at the large skyscraper, I got out of the car, letting my chauffeur know how long I'd be gone and telling him that he could return for me later. I glanced up at the glass windows and a perfectly etched font that proclaimed the building housed Autry Publishing, and I had a sinking feeling in the pit of my stomach. I couldn't tell whether it had been from excitement or fear. I was finally getting the chance to unleash my own expertise onto the world without being hounded by my father. I was also doing something that had never been done before by a member of any of the elite families I knew. Everyone liked to keep their secrets because it kept them powerful, but I was ready to air the necessary dirty laundry to get my point across—I didn't have to cut corners and trample over people's dreams in order to take the right risks and get to the top.

I entered the building and was immediately greeted by a lovely receptionist who took one look at me and asked if she could get me anything to drink. She led me right up to Preston's office, letting me know that he was going to be in at any moment. I glanced around at the various awards he'd gotten over the years, the shelves of books he'd published that he was most proud of, and the few articles that were written about him over the years. It was strange to be sitting here when I should've been at my own office taking care of business, trying to stay on top of all the changing things in my life without giving my parents any insight into what I was planning. Though it was much easier said than done, and there were always going to be times where something had to be put on the back burner, at least until I was sure that we had everything we needed to move the manuscript to the next step.

I kept looking over at the clock on the wall, realizing that this meeting had to be over in exactly an hour so that I could head down to the office in time to meet with my father and the board to discuss matters that he allowed me to be a part of. If I didn't show up, I knew he was going to find more reasons to try to cut me out of the important stuff, but my mind couldn't help but focus on the conversation I had with Eric outside my building. He seemed to know much more than he was letting on, and I was certainly not in the mood to be playing any games. I started this little endeavor of mine so that I wouldn't have to play games anymore, but I supposed that I'd find out everything I needed to know in due time.

It was times like these that I was overcome with fear and with the worry that I was getting into something that I'd have no control over, and I didn't want to think about what the repercussions would be if everything didn't go according to plan. I knew there were going to be a lot of angry businessmen waiting to have a word with me or crumble my budding business the minute I started making the right deals and sharing inside information into the things they never wanted to surface, but I had to be strong. I was doing this because I didn't want to live in the shadow of my father and because I believed that I could do a better job without all the underhanded business, but there was a part of me that was still operating in doubt.

I couldn't focus on that right now. Preston agreed to help me with this, and I was going to make sure that I saw it through. The door to the office swung open, and Preston came in with a to-go cup of coffee in his hands.

"I'm so sorry I'm late, Jamie. I had a few meetings before you, and I know you have to head off to work as soon as we're done. Do you have the manuscript?" he asked, settling down at his desk.

"It's a rough draft at best, but before I give it to you, I need your word that you're not going to share any of this information with anyone. The things written in this manuscript are going to hurt a lot of corporations and businesses owned by some of the richest people in the country, and if any of them find out about it before it's about to hit the shelves, they're going to do everything they can to stop it," I warned, and he nodded his head.

"When have I ever given you a reason to doubt me?" he asked. I stared back at him blankly, so he continued. "Your secret is safe with me, Jamie. Besides, this is exactly the kind of thing I've been looking to do for a while. I've been quite interested in the behind-the-scenes of lives like yours, and even like your beautiful friend, ah, Audrey, right?"

"Has she spoken to you about something she's writing?" I asked, genuinely curious.

"She's thrown around a few ideas, but she's also sworn me to secrecy until she has something concrete. She has a great way with words, and I know you two have been quite close lately, so if she's advising you at all, I think you're going to be in good hands," he said, and I couldn't agree more.

"She has big dreams. Just make sure she has everything she needs to succeed, okay? It's the least I can do for her," I said, and he nodded.

"She has genuine talent and great stories to tell. Though we're not here to talk about her. We're here to talk about you and your revolutionary exposé on the finance world of New York City with a little blue blood flair," he said, and I sighed.

"That's what it boils down to," I replied.

"Let's see what we're working with."

He read my manuscript, thumbing through every piece of advice I'd written, and when he finally looked up at me, he had a smile on his face. It didn't make me feel any better because I knew that regardless of that smile, he still could be ready to give me the heartbreaking criticism that would let me know I had no business trying to write a thing.

"You have good material here, Jamie. I do have to ask, though, are you sure that you want to go ahead with this, knowing there are chapters in here that will question your father's practices? I am on board with whatever you decide to do, but I just want you to know what the consequences could be for putting something like this out," he said, and I nodded my head.

"That book is going to help so many people get their start in the world, and they're finally going to be able to see behind my father's smokescreen. It isn't just about business-sense anymore. It's about trust, integrity, and risks. My father had countless chances to make a difference with the knowledge he has, but instead, he chose to keep it in his inner circles, breaking people down to get ahead, and it doesn't faze him. It's time something does," I said, and he nodded.

"Well, this is just the first stage. We still have a lot to do before this book is even remotely ready, and you still have writing you need to get done. I just want you to be careful. I know how ugly these things can get," he said, and I smiled politely at him.

"I'm well aware, but it's time someone said something. I've been trying to break away from my father's company for quite a while, and this is my chance to make a name for myself without him hovering over me. I learned a lot from him, there's no denying that, but I've also seen exactly the kind of man I want to avoid becoming. This is my way of telling the world that I have more to offer, and once this comes out, people are either going to turn a blind eye to me, or they're going to start taking me seriously. It's a risk I'm willing to take," I said.

"I'm proud of you. Just know, when your parents kick you out of the business entirely, call me. We'll have a drink," he said teasingly.

"You bet, man."

LEAVING THE AUTRY PUBLISHING BUILDING, I FELT LIKE a new man. I felt like I had just made the life-changing decision that was finally going to start giving my life purpose again. I knew it was merely a start, but I felt the urge to celebrate because I was one step closer to everything I'd wanted from the moment I realized I couldn't stand my father anymore. Though I knew that if I wanted to continue getting close to his underhanded business deals, I'd have to put myself front and center, going to the functions my mother organized so that I could keep a close eye on him to see what he was really up to. My father was the jack of all trades, and I was about to show him that I could do a much better job juggling different business ventures than he could've ever dreamed of. I wondered if there was a time he felt like me, wanting to break away from the family business, making a name for himself. I knew there was no way I'd ever know that because the Forrest name was far too important to him to think of anything or anyone else.

My mind averted back to sitting in that boardroom, watching him scramble to get himself together when he realized I was onto whatever he was trying to do and whatever he was trying to keep me out of. I couldn't understand why he repeatedly tried to keep me silent while I was working under him like another one of his employees. He forgot that I was his son and much more capable than anyone else he knew. For a while, I tried to convince myself that it was only because he expected the best of me. I tried to convince myself that he would eventually sit me down, have a drink with me, and tell me that he was proud of me. Now, I was well aware that that day was never going to come. It was quite possible both my parents were going to shun me entirely once the book went to press because they were going to feel the kind of betrayal and abandonment I'd felt my entire life, the kind of neglect that would make anyone go mad. The entire situation was starting to give me a headache because the more I thought about them, the more I began to loathe their existence.

I walked back to the town car I'd called moments before heading down to the lobby, trying not to think about the fact that the man I hated more than my father was going to be sitting in my parents' living room, along with my ex-girlfriend, and I still couldn't figure out why that was. My mother never liked Cece, nor did she care much for Eric because he was the one always dragging me out to parties, but it seemed that they had a change of heart. I suddenly felt a sinking feeling in my stomach like the meeting I'd had with Eric earlier had been a warning, and I began to wonder whether he was up to something terrible. I wouldn't put it past him. Ever since I banished him from the city for what he did, he told me to watch my back. It's quite possible he was finally making good on his threat.

I didn't want to think about it any longer, and I was in desperate need of a distraction, something to get me away from the chaotic life I lived. I decided to make a reservation down at a wonderful French restaurant not far from the heart of the city, hoping that Audrey would want to see me. I wanted to get to the bottom of why she'd been so distant lately, and I wanted to show her that she was the reason behind me finally being able to step out on my own. She opened my eyes to entirely new possibilities, and I needed to make sure she knew just how special she really is.

CHAPTER EIGHT: AUDREY

I hated that I'd been avoiding him, but I didn't know what else to do. I was scared that he'd only keep me close to finish this little business venture of his, and then he'd move on, getting back to his life and leaving me in the dust. I thought this through as I alphabetized the books that Henry had received that morning. He could tell that something was off with me, judging from the concern in his expression, but he didn't want to pry. I sighed, blowing up the strand of hair out of my face while I glanced down at my wristwatch to see how much time had passed already.

I was starting to feel rather antsy because I knew that Cece would be calling me any day now, telling me that she was back in town and that she needed that story the minute she landed. I had everything ready for her, but I wasn't sure about what was going to happen after. There was a part of me that wanted to abandon everything that I learned about that world, but I couldn't help how curious I was. I was starting to think that maybe I wanted to take a page out of Jamie's book and write about those who have piqued my interest the most, even if that meant having to get closer to them and their incessant, shallow behavior.

I still wondered whether I should call Jamie. I had my very first meeting with Preston Autry coming up to discuss a few of my stories and start the planning process for a new book that would be my debut as a published author. It was a lot to look forward to, but it also frightened me to the core. I knew that by taking on a subject such as writing about New York's elite, I could possibly dig myself so deep into a hole that no one would want much to do with me after that, but I couldn't help the intrigue that welled up inside of me whenever I tried to put it from my mind.

I had also been giving a lot of thought to what Claire had said. I had to decide if I wanted to continue spending time with Jamie, knowing that his head would always be elsewhere while he dealt with his dysfunctional family and broke out on his own while exposing them in the process. I wondered what I would do in that situation if given the opportunity to be that brave. I couldn't imagine speaking out against my family like that, even if it was the right thing to do.

I knew I had a lot of toughening up to do, especially if I wanted to get closer to these people, get inside their heads, and truly understand what it was like to live my life as one of them. That would be all I needed to start writing the story that could make my career and launch me into society as the writer I've always dreamed of becoming, but I had to be careful with who I decided to trust in the process.

I finished packing away the books, tended to the few customers that came trailing in through the door right before closing, and was getting ready to call it a night when I saw a familiar face appear in front of the cash register.

"Hello there. I'm looking for a book, something that will impress a girl I want to ask out to dinner yet again," Jamie said with his gorgeous smile plastered on his face.

I couldn't help but blush, and I was starting to realize that I was feeling things I couldn't describe, the kind of flutter in my stomach that made this entire situation that much more complicated.

"I'm sure I can find you something," I said, leading him to the back between the bookshelves while he inched closer to me. For a moment, I thought he was going to kiss me, and I had no idea what to think because up until that very point, I was avoiding him completely.

"You've been a little distant lately, and I know that I haven't been the best company lately, especially with everything going on in my life, but it's time I change that. I would like to take you out for dinner tonight and show you that there are parts of my world that aren't so bad. I can show you parts that can be quite lovely if you'll join me?" he asked, and I smiled back at him, unsure of how to decline such an offer.

"I've just been doing a lot of thinking, and I know you have so much to worry about. I didn't want to get in your way," I said, though there was much more to the story than that. I was starting to second-guess every single doubt I'd had over the last few days.

"You're never going to get in my way, Audrey. I love talking to you, I love spending time with you, and I want to show you that tonight. If you'll have me?" he asked again, and I chuckled.

"Oh, all right," I said with a smile, and I watched his face light up with excitement. Maybe Claire was wrong about him, after all. Maybe he was just one of the good ones.

I stoppED AT HOME to CHANGE, GETTING READy FOR the evening ahead. I came out in a tight-fitting red dress that hugged my curves in all the right places. Claire insisted that I buy it a few weeks ago when we went out shopping together, but I never thought that I would be wearing it out on a date with Jamie. He met me at the door like a gentleman, taking my hand in his as he led me back to his shiny, black town car.

"You look absolutely stunning," he said, smiling back at me while he held the door open.

"You don't look too bad yourself," I said, with a chuckle, sliding inside the backseat while he joined me.

We were well on our way to the restaurant when I noticed that something had been bothering him. No matter how much he tried to get out of his head for a little while, he was distracted. I felt bad, knowing how stressful everything must've been for him. I wanted to do whatever would help him feel a bit better.

"Are you all right?" I asked him.

"I'm fine, Audrey. It's been a rough couple of days, but I'm trying not to let everything going on deter me from living my life. It's been such a long time since I've actually taken the time to enjoy myself, and that's what I want tonight to be about," he said, and I smiled.

"I don't think you're going to be able to get very far with that until you get whatever is bothering you off your chest. I know I've been distant lately, and it's only because I didn't want to get in the middle of everything you're trying to do, but you have to know that I'm here for you, whenever you need," I said.

He reached down to grab my hand, squeezing it tightly. It was the first time I'd felt his touch at all, and it made my entire body light up with the kind of tingly excitement that I hadn't felt in a very long time.

"Remember when I told you that Cece cheated on me with my best friend?"

"Yes, I do," I said, nodding.

"He's back in town, and he's given me some sort of warning. I feel like he has something big up his sleeve, but I can't seem to figure out what that might be," he said.

Just like that, we were right back in the middle of the drama. It amazed me how everyone in his world was operating solely on trying to take each other down, and I couldn't help but fixate on characters like that, especially because it was so different from what I was used to.

"Has he given you any specifics?" I asked.

"Only that he's going to be at my parents' house tomorrow night with Cece at his side, as she's coming back in town. I don't want to deal with any of it, but I'm afraid the conversation might be exactly what I need to wrap up the book, especially if it has anything to do with business."

I stood there thinking for a moment, just as curious as he was about what they might be planning behind his back. "Would you like me to accompany you tomorrow evening? I'm sure it might help if you had a familiar face there to stand by you while you deal with all of them, especially because your relationships are never going to be the same after the book hits the shelves," I said, and he nodded.

"That would be amazing, Audrey. Thank you. I know that tonight was supposed to be about me taking you out to have a little fun and enjoy some of the finer things in life without me blabbing on about my problems, but things are finally going to change soon. The manuscript is nearing the finish line, and once it's done, I can get back to work that feels natural while waiting for it to hit the market like everyone else," he said, and I truly couldn't wait to see that day even though I was scared about what his parents' reaction might be.

I'd never been in the room with them or been around people that had so much power, and I was much more intimidated than I would've liked to be. The fact that someone of

Jamie's caliber would be trying to pull off such a risky deal scared me, but it also made me wonder what everyone else in his life was going to say about it. I wasn't sure he thought everything through completely, but then again, I knew absolutely nothing about the inner workings of his world. I had a feeling I was going to find out very soon, though. The entire evening, I couldn't get out of my head long enough to stop thinking about the man Jamie had mentioned, and I wondered if it was the same man I walked in on Cece kissing back at the party.

The thought of his agenda and what this all could be about made me want to find out more. It gave me the urge and the push I needed to want to write about such things, but I didn't think that Jamie would take too kindly to me writing about the people currently closest to him, even if he was planning on shutting them out himself. Though I thought that a few drafts wouldn't hurt, especially because I didn't think that it would get back to anyone. When Jamie finally dropped me home that evening, I sat at my computer, typing away everything that I had learned, and I began writing a story I'd never truly be able to tell the world.

CHAPTER NINE: JAMIE

I was at my desk in my suite early that morning, sipping lightly on two shots of espresso while I finished up the last of the manuscript before I turned it in to Preston. I had the chance to read it from beginning to end, and I was proud of the work I'd done and excited to share my knowledge with the world. I knew that it was going to change people's lives and their perceptions of what it actually takes to succeed, and I could only imagine that it was going to be the reason behind an eruption of chaos once the references to my father came to light. It was going to put a damper on my family's entire fortune, and I would finally be able to take the risks I needed without my father hovering over me, watching and dictating my every move. It felt good to have it finished. I knew I had to be in the office for a meeting with my father, so I decided to drop it off with the receptionist so that she could get it to Preston's office.

On the way to my building, I could've sworn I saw Eric hanging around outside in the courtyard again, but when I did a double-take, he seemed to disappear. I told myself that I was only a little too paranoid and that there was no way he was still here, but I didn't hold my breath because it wouldn't be too long before I had to face him and my entire family. I was just glad that Audrey said she would accompany me, especially after the way I'd been treating her. I didn't want this part of my life to consume her, especially when she still had so many dreams and so much ambition that she hadn't explored yet. I didn't want to be the one holding her back.

I was unable to shake the terrible feeling I had in the pit of my stomach, telling me that something awful was about to happen. I tried to put the thought from my mind, focusing on getting the work done for the day, so I wouldn't have to be in the office any longer than I had to. Though once I finally arrived and came up in the elevator, the receptionist was waiting there for me, looking as concerned as ever while she approached.

"Mr. Forrest has asked to see you in his office. He said that it's urgent," she said.

I had been wondering when he was going to do this, especially seeing as we hadn't spoken much outside of work since I crashed his meeting. I ventured off into his office, shutting the door behind me while I noticed that the rest of the room was empty. He had his assistant forward all his calls so he wouldn't be interrupted during our chat together.

"As my son, I expect you to behave the way that would best represent this family, but lately, all I've seen from you is disappointing behavior. Did you really think that I wouldn't find out about your extracurricular activities, Jamie? I know what you're trying to do, crashing my important meetings, talking back to your mother, and acting out like a child. You're not going to get the respect you think you deserve until you give me a single reason why I should even trust you. I expected better from you, and yet, you always seem to fall short," he said, and no matter how much hatred I had for him, it didn't make the words sting any less.

"I'm tired of living in your shadow, Father. I'm sure you barely even remember what that feels like. I deserve more responsibility around here, but you refuse to give it to me, so of course I'm acting out. I act out because it's the only way to get through to you and Mother. It's the only way you two respond to anything that doesn't involve your precious empire. You two are a colossal disappointments to me, and I'm sorry, but it's not going to be that way forever," I warned, letting him know in very little words that I was planning on leaving him and his company in the dust.

"Watch your mouth, Jamie. You have no idea who you're dealing with here, and if you want to continue living your life with all the luxuries you currently have, I suggest you start thinking about what the consequences of your actions are going to be. I built this business because I wanted a way to dabble in every opportunity that caught my eye, and I've learned to take risks and pay my dues in ways you can't possibly imagine. Whatever you think you have planned, it's going to have to come to a screeching halt. Otherwise, you're going to lose everything you have. If you think that you're going to walk out that door, go find another board of investors to take you in and let you lead them, you're sadly mistaken. I own everyone around here, and they all answer to me whether they like it or not. At this rate, you're never going to have that, Jamie. It really is such a shame," he said, and his words cut through me like a knife, taking all of my insecurities and laying them on the table in front of him.

"You're the one that needs to watch your back, Father. You have no idea what's coming, and eventually, you won't have a wall to hide behind," I warned, and he shook his head.

"Be on time for dinner, son. We have a lot to discuss when you arrive, and I suggest you take what I said into consideration because you're treading on a thin line here, Jamie," he said, and I got up, ready to storm out the door, but he stopped me. "Oh, and don't bring that boring brunette you've been seeing. She isn't your type, and she's never going to fit in around here. Don't be fooled, son. You're never going to have a normal life, and I still don't understand why you want it so bad. She is never going to love you when she sees the man you really are. You have to find someone of your standards, someone that would stick by you no matter what terrible decisions you have to make, but you'll find that out soon enough," he said.

I couldn't believe the words that came out of his mouth.

I couldn't focus much on work after that, so I headed home early, feeling my stomach turn at the thought of what he was going to hit me with later that evening. I wanted to call Audrey and call the entire thing off, but everything inside was telling me to hold on. I knew something like this could happen when I decided to start this endeavor. Now, I had to see it through. I remembered why I'd taken it this far in the first place. If I wanted people to start taking me seriously, I was going to have to take this risk, no matter what the consequences were going to be. I thought back to all the times when I'd let myself slip in the past, when my mind and body were working against me, and when I drank myself sick every night trying to numb the pain inside.

Now, I had a different feeling coursing through me. I was fuelled with anger, waiting for the right moment to tell my father that he wasn't going to keep me locked down and use me as his little errand boy any longer. He was so good at convincing everyone that my abilities were much less than they actually were, and it was time everyone got a good look into how these empires were truly built. It was then that I realized I was doing the right thing and that any advice that I could give the general public would help because it would make everyone see that it shouldn't have to be this way. My father shouldn't be able to command people the way he has, and it was time someone gave the rest of the world a fair chance. I wanted to be the driving force behind that, and I knew that once my name was plastered on the front cover of that book, my entire life was going to change.

I didn't understand how he knew about Audrey, and it dawned on me that he probably had people watching over me this entire time, gathering as much information as they possibly could to report back to him. I could only hope that they didn't catch wind of the book, because if I had lost that opportunity, I didn't know if I'd ever have the chance to break away again. I knew I had to warn Audrey about what she was about to walk into because I didn't want her to be blind-sided by anything that my family would say. I knew they didn't like her and that they thought she was below me, but they had no idea what they were talking about. They wouldn't know genuine if it slapped them in the face, and I needed to make sure that she and I were on the same page.

I heard the landline ring, and I answered it as the receptionist asked if Audrey could be sent up. I said yes. I waited there for the door to open while I tried to calm the pounding of my heart in my chest. I truly felt like it was going to explode. The moment she came in, she could read the expression on my face, and she knew there was trouble. She inched closer to me, caressing my cheek while she waited for me to tell her what was going on. It felt so good to feel her touch and support. She could've taken the deal I gave her with Preston and forgotten all about me, but she stuck around despite how consuming my life had been. I didn't know how to properly thank her for all of that. Though I knew it would have to be at another time. I sat her down on the chaise lounge in my sitting room and told her everything my father had said instead.

"Wow, he's a dick. My apologies. I know he's your father," she said.

"Trust me, he is a dick. I don't know what we're going to be walking into, but whatever it is, I can assure you that it isn't good. I would understand if you wanted to back out, especially after what he said about you. I don't want you to ever be treated that way. You deserve so much more than that. You deserve better than me, Audrey," I said.

The words hurt coming out of my mouth because I realized that I had begun to have true feelings for her. I knew that I would never be good for her and that my life was far too complicated for her to get involved, but she looked me deep in my eyes and shook her head at me like she wasn't about to take in what I'd said.

"I care about you, Jamie. I don't care that your family might have a few choice words to say about me. What I care about is being there for you and showing you that you have the support you need. You have to decide how to move forward with this because, as far as you know, they have no idea what your plans are. That manuscript of yours is a smoking gun," she said, and I couldn't agree more.

"I don't think I can back out of it now. I made my decision. I just hope that it doesn't cost me every opportunity I'd been working for my entire life. I really appreciate you being here with me, Audrey. I don't know how I would've been able to cope without you," I said.

My eyes lowered to her lips. At that moment, all I wanted to do was kiss her. I knew it was selfish, and I knew that she absolutely did deserve much better than me, but I couldn't stop myself. She inched closer to me, and I leaned in, pressing my lips to hers. My body erupted with a need for her that I never expected to feel. She made me feel so much better as she stood by me and put up with my terribly chaotic life even though she surely didn't have to.

"You're such an amazing woman, Audrey. I don't know what I would've done if you weren't here," I said as she took my face into the palm of her hands, caressing my cheeks ever so lightly.

"What matters is that I'm here, and whatever happens tonight, I'm still going to be right here with you," she said, and I smiled.

I helped her into her coat, we both took a deep breath, and we were off. The drive to my parents' house was silent. I wanted nothing more than to turn back around and pretend like nothing was going to happen, but I knew that wasn't the right thing to do. I had to face the music no matter how much it was going to rattle me because that was the kind of man I wanted to be. I didn't want to be the kind of man that ran away from my problems and blamed everyone else for my shortcomings when I knew good and well that I wasn't perfect. I just hated dragging Audrey into all of this, no matter how much she'd convinced me that she wanted to be here.

I couldn't deny that my feelings for her were growing, even if I did believe that once she got in the room alone with both of my parents, she would certainly have enough to want to leave. My father certainly didn't think that she'd be able to handle all of the terrible things that went on in my world, and I was starting to fear that he may have been right. She always put up such a brave front, but I knew deep down that she must've been questioning whether getting involved with me was the right decision or not. Whatever happened from here on out certainly wouldn't be easy, but if she decided to stay, I truly believed that I would be able to make it through.

Finally, the car pulled in through the wrought-iron gates around my parents' mansion. It'd been such a long time since

I remembered actually enjoying my time spent at their house because it was the very place that I'd done some of the worst things I could think of—things that my parents liked to reference whenever I was getting out of hand. My heart was beating so loudly that it was drowning out the sounds of everything else, and I gulped, opening up the door and holding it open so that Audrey could get out with me. She looked absolutely stunning, and it was the first time I was able to see that she truly did appear like she belonged here. If my father didn't know where she came from, I'm sure he wouldn't have even batted an eye. Though, at this point, he was going to use everything he could think of against me until I acted the way he wanted and until I was operating solely on his time and his decisions.

We rang the doorbell, and the door swung open to reveal my mother in her expensive dress and glistening pearls, which she clutched in her hands the moment she realized that I wasn't alone. She greeted me kindly, completely ignoring Audrey's presence, and I could tell that Audrey was a bit hurt by the lack of exchange. I squeezed her hand tightly, and she nodded, letting me know that she was going to be okay.

"Come along, Jamie. You must be starving," my mother said.

I led Audrey into the lavish dining room, where she sat down next to me. I glanced over at my father at the head of the table, who barely bothered to acknowledge either of us.

"I thought I told you not to bring her here," he said, sipping lightly on his glass of water.

"I decided that I didn't have to listen to you. I care about Audrey, and you as my parents are going to have to deal with that," I said, watching my mother take her seat.

We waited patiently for a few moments until the doorbell rang again. In came Cece with Eric on her arm, and to my surprise, his father and mother were with him. It was strange to see them there, and my heart sank into my stomach when I realized that something big was about to go down.

I glanced over at Audrey and shrugged my shoulders because I truly had no idea what was about to happen. Everyone seemed to be quite calm for the time being, and I could only hope that it would stay that way. Cece had a large grin on her face until she caught sight of me sitting next to Audrey, and then her face soured immediately.

"What the hell are you doing here?" she asked, not even trying to be subtle.

"Jamie invited me. What are you doing here?" Audrey asked, matching the same dry tone as Cece.

"I'm here to accompany Eric. It's a big night for him. The coming together of two families in an incredible business venture is a celebration, but I'm sure your parents are going to fill you in after the main course, Jamie," she said, winking at me. I couldn't help but feel like I was about to be sick.

They all sat down at the table, and my mother leaned over Cece's shoulder, whispering something to her while her eyes finally found me. She looked so incredibly disappointed, but she tried to hide it behind a smile even though we all knew that something terrible was going to happen the minute the plates were finally cleared. I felt Audrey's hand reach under the table, resting on mine in support, and I was so glad that she was there with me, though I knew it was hard for her.

I could see it in her eyes that she was trying her best to swallow the pain and the hurt of not even being acknowledged by my family, and it only made me hate them that much more. I wanted to put them all in their places, but I knew I couldn't do that until I found out what they'd been waiting to tell me. This entire dinner was an ambush, that was as much as I could tell right now. I struggled to get my food down while Audrey finished hers.

I watched Cece get up from her seat and drag Audrey away into the bathroom, and I knew she was going to have a field day tearing Audrey apart. I could only hope that she wasn't going to be too hurt and that she wasn't going to storm out of here with tears in her eyes. I knew just how vindictive Cece could be when she wanted to. I sighed, watching both of my parents keep their eyes on me while they engaged in polite chit-chat with Eric's parents. Eric had a grin on his face from the time he came strolling in through the front door, and I could already sense that I was the only one that was going to be hurt by what would be said after dessert.

The night dragged on longer than I could've imagined, and I was expecting the girls to be back by now, but they were nowhere to be seen. I thought that maybe it was Eric's doing, making sure that I didn't have any distractions when I was finally hit with the news. My mother led us all into the study where she was getting ready to serve us after-dinner drinks, and my stomach was turning so badly that I thought I was going to throw up. I held myself together in an attempt to show everyone in the room that whatever they could say to me wouldn't faze me in the slightest. Then my father decided to speak up, and the part of the night I'd been dreading most finally began.

"I'd like to thank you all for being here on this joyous occasion. It's not often that I agree to join forces with anyone, and this truly is the start of something extraordinary. I never thought that I would see the day Forrest Industries joins the Richfields, but today is that day. It's quite an amazing story, how my son here was off plotting his schemes and trying to undermine my success while I've had a plan of my own in the works for quite some time. Would you like to say anything, Jamie?" my father asked.

I knew he could already see the disappointment in my eyes and how terrible I had been feeling inside at the thought of Eric's family getting anywhere near the family business. It was exactly the kind of thing that would make me want to stay, and I was finding it hard to see myself getting out of this now, but I knew I had to be strong. I'd come too far to just give up all hope now.

"I have nothing to say to you, Father. You must've gone soft if you need someone else to help you out, damaging the Forrest name by joining forces. Haven't you learned anything over the years? Oh, that's right, all you do is step on people to get ahead, and for the first time ever, you're allowing them to step all over you. I want no part in this, and there is nothing that you can say to make me stay," I said, and he shook his head, heading over to one of the shelves to retrieve the envelope that had been sitting proudly there.

"Even this?" he asked, throwing it down on the table in front of me.

I took it into my hands, opening it up to find my manuscript inside. "Where the hell did you get this?" I asked, angrily.

"Your friend Preston accepted a generous donation to his company when he gave up the information about your plans to expose our business practices. I say, this is probably the worst attempt at acting out that you've ever enacted, son. I'm very disappointed in you, but this is your chance to make it up to me. Without that book of yours, you have no choice but to try to make amends. You have to do right by your family the way we've always done right by you," he said, and I shook my head, fuming to the point where I nearly threw my glass into the fireplace.

"You have to be out of your mind if you think I'm going

to stick around and watch you burn Forrest Industries to the ground. I'm going to do just fine on my own," I said, even though I had a hard time believing my own words now.

"I beg to differ, Jamie. One, you are under contract—a contract that you signed one night when you were too drunk to remember in the attempt to make me trust you again. It states that under no circumstances are you allowed to exploit Forrest Industries or this family, but I don't think that you remember that. I mean, why would you? You were drunk out of your mind. Though you're going to have to start getting your act together because I'm not always going to be around to clean up your messes and stop you from making terrible mistakes," he said, and I glanced around at every pair of eyes in the room as they all silently judged me.

"I don't need this. I'll find my way out of this contract, I will pack my things, and I will get out of here," I said, gritting my teeth.

"And where exactly will you go, Jamie? I made sure that no reputable business in the country will touch you. You're stuck, son. I'm sorry that it has to be this way, but there was no other option apart from backing you into a corner. You're going to see someday, and you'll be thanking me."

"Go to hell, Father," I said, grabbing my coat right before I stormed out.

I caught sight of Eric's stupid grin, and I did what I felt was right at the moment. I punched him straight in the lip for the way he was looking at me. It left a trace of blood on my knuckle, but I didn't care. It felt good, and it made me feel better.

Where was Audrey? We had to get out of here, and I wasn't going to leave without her.

CHAPTER TEN: AUDREY

W hat the hell was going on? I needed to get back to Jamie. I could only imagine how much they must've been ripping into him right now. I stared back at Cece while she fixed her lipstick in one of the mirrors of the master bathroom. She dragged me all the way upstairs, but any time I tried to leave, she stood in front of the door, not offering me much of an explanation.

"You have some nerve showing up here with him. You do realize that there's no way he's actually into you, right? He was just using you to help him with his project, but his father saw to it to make sure that stupid book was never going to see the light of day. So, he's going to be back to his old self in no time, and you're not going to want to be around when that goes down," she said, pursing her lips together as she tousled her hair with her fingers.

"What the hell are you talking about? How does he even know about the book?" I asked.

"Oh, you have a lot to learn about how things work around here, little one. Preston has been a friend of all of ours for a very long time, and he was given an offer he couldn't refuse, so he gave Mr. Forrest a copy of the manuscript. Mr. Forrest was absolutely livid the moment he realized what Jamie's plans were, and I can only imagine it was the reason behind him wanting to join forces with the Richfields. Jamie would never want to see Eric get any sort of power, so he's going to stick around, be a good son to his parents, and finally stop wasting time with lowlifes like you. You have no place here, and I hate the fact that my mother agreed to run the story that you wrote. Oh, that's right, I told her to cut it from the issue. You don't get your happy ending because you don't belong here, and you can kiss any publishing deal you had with Preston goodbye. I suggest you get out of here. Once they finish up with Jamie, I'm quite sure he's never going to want to see you again," she said, and she almost brought me to tears.

I couldn't believe how much her words hurt or the lengths that everyone went to in order to keep Jamie in his place. It made me sick to know that they weren't going to let him go and that he was going to have to pretend that everything could somehow go back to normal when any sliver of freedom he had was now taken away from him. I knew he had been tired of living like that for a very long time, and I could only imagine that it would make him go on a bender when he found out he might not be able to claw his way out of this. I wanted to be there for him. I wanted to comfort him, but there was a part of me that was afraid that Cece might be right. If he really was going to be stuck in this world with nowhere to go, it was quite possible that he was going to realize he wanted nothing to do with me anymore. He would need to find a girl that was up to both his and his parents' standards.

"I hope you enjoyed your little fairytale while it lasted. It's over now, and so is any chance you had at happiness with Jamie," she said.

I pushed past her, storming out of the room and heading downstairs to see Jamie standing there waiting for me. I felt the hot tears begin to stream down my face, and I was sure I had never been so angry in my entire life. Every opportunity I'd been given and every dream I had was taken away from me in a matter of minutes, and unlike Jamie, I couldn't just snap my fingers and get them back.

"Let me take you home," he said, trying to embrace me, but I couldn't handle it.

"No. I'm going to call a cab. You have too much to deal with here. You should stay. I'm so sorry, Jamie," I said to him, fully crying now while I ran out onto the driveway.

I walked through the gates, clutching my coat around my shoulders as I hailed a cab. I didn't even bother to turn back, and once I was safely inside the vehicle, I realized that Jamie didn't even try to stop me. Maybe it was all too good to be true, after all.

I WAS STILL CRYING WHEN I GOt HOME AND SLAMMED my front door as I tossed my coat onto the couch, and Claire came out of her room. She wore an expression of deep concern, but I wasn't in the mood to divulge all of the details right then. I was too frustrated and too scared by what I had seen and what I had lost. I wished I never would've accompanied Jamie there tonight. I had no idea what I was walking into when I had agreed.

"What happened?" she asked, sitting me down on the couch, trying to calm me down.

"It's all over, Claire. Jamie, my story, the publishing deal. It's all gone, just like that," I said through my tears.

"That's not possible!" she screamed angrily.

I filled her in on every little detail from the night. It was a night that shook me to my core and filled me with the kind of rage I'd never felt before. I wished I could return to a time when I didn't know about any of this and when I was trying to make my way, wide-eyed and full of dreams. Now, I couldn't help but feel overwhelmed by the number of opportunities I'd lost, along with a budding relationship that probably wouldn't have lasted anyway. What was I thinking, getting involved with a man like Jamie while knowing where he came from and knowing who he was involved with? I felt terrible that he was backed into a corner and couldn't live out his dreams the way he wanted to, but I was much more concerned about how this was going to affect me.

I was on my way to having everything I had dreamed of, and I didn't know how to cut my losses and move on. My world felt like it was crumbling down around me, and I had no idea how to build it back up while knowing that I was probably never going to get another opportunity like that again. I was about to have my name in a magazine and on the cover of a book that would've been sold in the very bookstore I worked at, and now all of that was taken away from me. I cried myself to sleep that night on the couch, clutching the blanket that Claire had brought over for me. She tried to get me to drink a cup of tea and eat something, but I refused. I was far too distraught to think about anything else. I laid there, hoping I was going to wake up from this terrible nightmare.

When morning finally came, I had to get myself together so I could go to work. I had to dry my tears and make myself look somewhat presentable while I tried to figure out how I was going to move forward. Claire had tried her best, and I was so grateful that she was there with me because I knew I couldn't do it without her. She made me breakfast, and I ate with her in complete silence, bidding her a soft goodbye before heading out the door to make my way to Greer's. I had to keep myself from crying all day, and any moment that my thoughts returned to anything about Jamie, I had to stop it in its tracks before it overwhelmed me again. I didn't know if I was ever going to see him again or if he even cared to see me after what happened. His parents had given him an ultimatum, and I couldn't imagine he would ever try to defy them for my sake. They took away his golden ticket to freedom, and I was just collateral damage caught in the middle of it all.

I clutched my chest, trying to ease the pain as I entered the bookstore, and Henry could immediately tell that something was wrong. He told me to take it easy and not rush things today because he could tell that I needed a break. I thanked him for being so kind even though I certainly didn't deserve it. I nearly abandoned him the moment I got an offer I couldn't refuse, and it dawned on me that I was a lot more like the people in Jamie's world than I may have thought. I didn't want to sit around all day and feel sorry for myself. I needed something to fixate on that would help to take the pain away and give me something to look forward to, but I didn't know what would help.

On my break, Henry came over to me with what appeared to be an old leather-bound journal in his hands. He gave it to me with a comforting smile, following it up with a pen so that I could pour my heart out onto the page.

"Some of the greatest grief turns into the best stories. It may help if you remember your outlet, just like half the writers on these shelves," he said with a smile.

"Thank you very much, Henry. This truly does mean a lot," I responded. I felt the slight trickle of a single tear roll down my face as I took it from him.

"I may not know what's bothering you, but I can guess it has something to do with that handsome fellow I see in here from time to time. Just know that whatever you feel like you've lost, it's only temporary. You will find happiness again. I can guarantee it," he said.

"How can you be so sure?"

"I read a lot of books," he said, and I chuckled.

It was the first time I'd uttered a genuine laugh since everything had happened, and it made me feel good. I still had a few minutes left of my break, so I cracked open the journal he'd given me and started writing about all of the things I'd experienced over the last twenty-four hours. I felt so much better after I was done. I was writing a story that felt genuine and was all my own. It felt good to focus on myself and doing what I loved for a change without feeling the need to impress anyone along the way. I had started to feel a certain rush of adrenaline course through me, similar to how I felt when Cece had first offered me the job. This didn't have to be the end of the story for me. This could be the beginning, and nothing was going to stop me from telling this story my way. I realized that I could make my own opportunity here. I could pick up where Jamie left off and write the story that would give everyone an inside look into how the people in his world really operated.

It was going to break a lot of boundaries, and I could only imagine that Jamie would be furious if he ever found out, but I didn't care. I wanted to do this for me. I wanted back into that world so I could explore it for myself. I could have a firsthand look at every nasty thing those people say and do, giving a voice to the outsider for once. I fixated on the idea, trying to figure out how I was going to pull it off, and that's when I realized I had quite a bit of writing to do. If Cece saw my writing and said that it was good enough that she wanted to hire me, there had to be someone else out there that might feel the same way about this story. It was possible that I could send in submissions to a few magazines and publishing houses, throwing around the idea until something clicked. It was worth a shot, and I really didn't have anything to lose.

I started to perk up around closing time, and just as I finished locking up, I felt a presence behind me. It was someone I certainly didn't expect to see again.

"Hello, Audrey," he said, looking as distraught as ever.

"Hi, Jamie," I said, trying not to hold his gaze. I felt hurt by everything we were both going through, and I didn't want him to see it.

"I know you probably don't want to see me right now. Cece clued me in on what she told you, and right now, I don't know what else I can do. My father ambushed me and backed me into a corner, and I have no choice now but to play by his rules. Though he's wrong about you. You are the best thing that's happened to me in a very long time, Audrey. I can't remember the last time I felt genuine happiness until you came into the picture, and I don't want to lose that. I know you lost a lot of things, too, and I'm not going to deny that. I wish I could help you further, but I'm afraid of the same thing happening again," he said, and I hung onto every word he said, trying to figure out if there was a way that we could meet in the middle of all of this.

"There is a way that you can help me, Jamie," I said firmly.

"What? I'll do anything."

"You can let me back into your world so that I can gather enough information on the people who hurt you and took your freedom away from you. I can write the book that will expose them for who they truly are. I don't have anything to lose like you do, and this way, everyone will get their chance in the limelight," I said.

I watched as the gears turned behind his eyes while he gave it some thought. For a moment, I thought he was going to stick up for them. I thought he would say no because, deep down, he didn't want to see them hurt, but he surprised me with his answer.

"Audrey Harlow, I truly don't know what I would do without you. If you're willing to do that, then I am more than willing to help you. You deserve this, and I promise to stand right by your side, even if things get more complicated than either of us realize. I'm so sorry that this turned out the way it did, but if it's an entrance into my world that you're looking for so that you can gather the dirt you need, I will do whatever I can to help," he said, and I smiled.

"Well, then it's settled. I will get started on my research right away, and I will take that manuscript to someone that isn't ruled by your father's wishes, so the rest of the world can get an inside look into what it's really like being a part of this world," I said, and he nodded.

"You truly are a fighter, Audrey. I admire that about you. You've gone after what you want ever since I met you, and I can't wait to see where you take this. I know that we're going to have a tough time, especially when everyone in my life realizes that you're not going anywhere, but I promise to make it as painless as possible," Jamie said.

"Don't worry, Jamie, I can take care of myself. I have to thank you for coming back and showing me that, despite everything that has happened, your intentions are pure," I said, and he inched closer to me. I could feel the heat of his skin brush against mine, and I knew what was coming next.

"I think we're going to make quite the team, Audrey. Don't you?"

"I think so, too," I said.

His eyes lowered to my lips, and I felt them press into mine. It ignited something inside me that I simply couldn't put into words. I melted into him, feeling his arms wrap around me, pulling me closer while he kissed me passionately. The past twenty-four hours had been a roller coaster of emotions, but together, I truly believed we were going to turn this unfortunate situation into something revolutionary. It was going to take time, and it was going to put a strain on our budding relationship, but if there was one thing I knew for sure, it was that Jamie wasn't like the people in his life. He had a big heart, and I genuinely believed that this was going to change us both for the better. It was going to be quite the adventure from here on out, that was for sure.

CHAPTER ELEVEN: JAMIE

*E*verything I'd done and everything that I'd worked for over the past few months was snatched away from me. My parents made sure to leave no stone unturned, and I felt that they would call the shots for the rest of my life. It was as if someone had taken me back to the time when my father was just starting to involve me in the family business and when I couldn't seem to get my act together despite how much everyone was telling me that they believed in me.

I was moping around my suite when I heard the landline ring. It was the receptionist telling me that I had a visitor, but I didn't feel like seeing anyone at the time.

"Tell whoever it is that I'm not home," I said.

"He's insisting, sir. He says that it's an urgent business matter that can't wait," she said, and I sighed.

It never ends, does it?

"Okay, send him up," I instructed, slamming the phone down and wishing I didn't have to entertain Eric after everything that he'd done to screw up my entire life.

"You're supposed to be at work," was the first thing that

came out of his mouth when he came strolling through the door.

"Did I not tell you to leave me alone? It's bad enough that our families have joined forces, but do you really have to be around all the time?" I asked, feeling rather annoyed by just seeing his face.

"I let the punch slide, Jamie. I know you remember that there was a time that we were friends. I've apologized countless times for screwing that up, but it doesn't have to be that way forever. You're going to see, man. We all did you a favor by hosting that little intervention to get your head out of your ass," he said.

I scoffed, pouring myself a glass of Scotch, which I would need while I listened to him whine on about everything else he was going to criticize about me. "If you're so sorry for what happened between us, then why would you think to threaten me the moment you came back into town? Why would you come to my parents' home with Cece on your arm, knowing that's a tender subject for me? I don't think that I'm a bad friend in this situation, Eric. You have a lot of soul searching to do."

He looked down at the floor, and for a moment, I could see a sense of guilt in his expression.

"I'm not proud of my actions, Jamie. I was angry after the way we left things, but that doesn't mean I ever stopped caring about you. This is an incredible opportunity for everyone involved, and since we are going to be working alongside each other, it's probably best that we start getting along. Besides, aren't you looking forward to the little celebratory party our mothers are organizing to tell the world what our plans are?" he asked, genuinely curious if there was even a sliver of me that was excited for any of this.

"You have to be out of your mind if you think this is even remotely a good thing. I hate that I have no say in any of this and that I'm just supposed to go about the rest of my life doing the bare minimum until it's time for me to take over Forrest Industries. That's not how I wanted my life to go. That is not how I wanted to spend the better half of my adult years. I spent far too long getting wasted with you when I should've been focusing on how to get out from under my father's grasp. Now, even that choice has been taken away from me, and I'm not happy about any of it," I said, and he looked incredibly surprised to hear me be this honest with him.

"Look, man. I know things are difficult right now, but they're not always going to be this way. You'll see that you're capable of so much more and that your father is going to give you the opportunities you want when he thinks you're ready. Has there been not a single doubt in your mind? Have you not thought that maybe you weren't going to make it out there on your own? You were born with opportunities, Jamie. Don't throw them away. Make them worth something," Eric said, and I knew he was always good at manipulating people, but I never thought that I would find myself actually considering what he'd said.

"I don't think I can do that, Eric. Unfortunately, I don't have much of a say in the matter, and I'd really appreciate it if you didn't try to convince me that this is somehow a blessing in disguise. You came here to tell me that I should get back to work, so let me go and do that while you walk your ass right out the front door," I said.

He didn't say another word, only turning around to leave. I didn't think our relationship was ever going to be the same, no matter how hard he tried to convince me that he was just looking out for me all along. I knew enough to realize that he had to have an ulterior motive and that this little visit back into town was going to mark the beginning of a very difficult time for the Forrest family. If my father did this to prove a point, he was going to have to be the one to deal with the consequences. That would be difficult considering how much my father hated to share.

I spent the rest of the day catching up on work because I couldn't imagine wasting any more time knowing that my father was going to try to undermine me again. I knew that nothing I did was ever going to be good enough for him, and I was incredibly tired of having him breathe down my neck about all the things I'd been doing wrong over the years. He went to extreme lengths to keep me where I was, making sure that no matter what I did, I could never leave the company. I had yet to find out why that was.

As evening neared, I glanced down at my wristwatch to check the time. I got into the back of my black town car and drove down to Greer's to pick up Audrey. She'd been busy lately, with all the writing she'd been doing, juggling work, and dealing with everything that happened with the story for Cece. I feel like I'd barely seen her. I was worried that the closer she got to my world and the more involved she got while trying to do as much research as possible, the more it was going to consume her.

I was well aware of the toll that living a life like mine could have on someone, and I didn't want Audrey to ever hate the person she becomes because I'd certainly been there at different points in my life. There were times I was so sure I wasn't going to be able to bounce back and that there would be nothing to save me from myself, yet I continued to dig myself deeper into a hole that my parents had to free me from.

Audrey was strong, and she'd been resilient ever since we had that conversation outside of the bookstore, where she told me she was going to write a book all about the people in my life. I thought about how terrible it could be for everyone around me, and I just couldn't wait for the day when I could finally see everyone around me crumble, paying for what they took from me. I had to be on my best behavior for the time being. Otherwise, my father was going to find yet another creative way to punish me for my actions, and if there was one thing he knew how to do well, it was to hurt me.

He'd been criticizing me my whole life, and there was a time when I accepted that criticism because I truly thought it was coming from a place of tough love. The older I got, though, the more I realized that he just hated my guts. He wanted me to be the one to carry on his legacy, not make one of my own. That was evidently clear when he took my manuscript, the book that I had poured my heart and soul into, only to stop it in its tracks and tear my hopes and dreams away from me. He wasn't going to allow his only son to be the one standing in the way of his success.

I still had to pay Preston a visit to beat him to the ground for breaking our agreement. I never thought that he'd be the kind of person to accept money from my father, knowing good and well what the angle of the book had been and how it was going to change lives. If I'd had a single doubt about his intentions, I would've taken my book elsewhere. Now that story was lost to the public. No one was going to hear anything from my perspective anymore. It wasn't about changing the world now. It was about getting revenge.

I saw the glimmer in Audrey's eyes the moment she told me she was going to be working on a story that exposed all of the terrible people in my life, and I could only hope that determination wouldn't get the best of her. I promised myself that I would protect her at all costs because if there was one thing my family was extremely good at, it was ruining people's lives. I couldn't let that happen to Audrey, not after everything she'd been through. She had been the only thing that kept me going this long, and I didn't know what I would do if I didn't have her by my side. She gave me hope that I wouldn't have to live like this forever and that there would be a way out of that pesky contract my father made me sign. I couldn't imagine that he managed to get the document drawn up perfectly, covering all of his bases while leaving no room for loopholes.

I knew that if I was going to get my revenge and make my family pay for everything they'd done, I had to be smart. I had to lay in wait and find a golden opportunity that no one would be able to take away from me.

EPILOGUE: AUDREY

I t's so strange for me to have one foot in my old life and the other in Jamie's world of elitist socialites and shady businessmen. There is a part of me that's worried I'm going to let it swallow me whole. I fear that getting close to all the luxuries is going to get to my head and turn me into a completely different person, but I can only hope that doesn't happen. I have to be strong, I have to write this story, and I have to show the world what's hiding behind each and every one of their façades.

I sat at the edge of my bed, thinking about where this journey was going to take me. I couldn't help but allow myself to feel everything as it hit—the realization that I was going to have to play the part if I wanted to be in this. I didn't know if I had what it took to be convincing while I interacted with these people as though I understood their world, but I had Jamie.

In such a short amount of time, he'd made me feel things that I had never experienced before. My heart would flutter at the mention of his name, when I knew that he was outside my door, or when he pulled up to Greer's to pick me up at the end of my shift. Part of this situation felt like a fairytale. I felt like I was being whisked away by a handsome prince who was going to change my life forever, but it was far more complicated than that. The life he lived was a complicated one, and there weren't many people in his life that understood him or gave him the opportunity to be himself.

His parents pressured him into signing a contract that would dictate the rest of his life if he didn't find a way out of it, and the one chance he had to expose their ways was snatched away from him, much like the opportunities he'd given me. I was beginning to see just how fake they all were. They all pretended to be the people they weren't, and I decided right then that there wasn't anyone apart from Jamie who I could trust. I didn't know how far I'd have to get in all of this before I felt satisfied enough to bring the story to a close, but I was fuelled with anger, frustration, and the need to get all of my emotions out onto paper.

I saw how different Jamie had become since he was roped back into his old life. He was spending more time with me and doing just about anything for an escape because heading back home or back to the office was too much for him to handle at times. I wanted to be his escape, but my biggest fear was that he was eventually going to get sucked back into the things he once enjoyed about his life, forgetting that I existed along the way. His father had some choice words to say about me, where I came from, and my lack of potential. Cece made sure that I understood that I would never be right for Jamie, no matter how much he convinced me that he cared. Even though I knew her words came from a place of jealousy, I was worried that there might be some truth underneath.

She'd known him much longer than I had, and she'd seen sides of him that I didn't know about. Jamie and I still had a lot to explore together, and the first jab at his family was going to be the party to celebrate the bringing together of the

Forrest and the Richfield families, which Jamie invited me to attend. I wanted to look the part and make an impact on those in the room so that they would remember me. That was the only way I was going to start climbing the ranks myself—by showing them all I still had what it took to exist in their world even if I wasn't born into money. They truly believed that they were invincible and that they would be able to shut down any threat that came their way. They may have gotten to Preston and stolen Jamie's ticket out, but they had no idea what I was up to.

I was going to tell each and every one of their stories exactly as it played out before my eyes, and there would be nothing anyone could do to stop it. I was surprised that Jamie wanted to help me at all, but he seemed to have enough anger coursing through him that all he wanted was revenge. He was so tired of being pushed around that he would do anything to be able to break out on his own and be taken seriously as his own man instead of another one of his father's employees. It was only a matter of time before we both got too deep and were in each other's hair so much that things got complicated. I knew how challenging this could be for both of us, especially seeing as we were trying so hard to keep our heads above water.

It was an overwhelming experience no matter what angle you looked at it from, and I just hoped I wouldn't allow the good parts of myself to be lost in all of this. They were all I had left to hold onto. Without them, I wouldn't recognize myself, and I was sure that Jamie wouldn't find the same interest in me that he'd had when we first met. It was going to be quite the adventure for us both, and I was both excited and downright terrified to see where it was going to take us next.

The first step would be to establish myself in society and show everyone that I could look, act, and speak just as they did. I had to learn to blend in with the crowd, making sure I stayed out of sight when I needed to. I was going to gather information, get under their skin, and make sure that their terrible behavior was brought to light when the book finally hit the shelves.

This was my opportunity to fight back for everything that was taken away from me. It was my chance to do right by Jamie. I just hoped that I made the right decision, and this was not something I would regret for the rest of my life.

PART II

CHAPTER ONE: JAMIE

My life had gotten so much more complicated, and I now woke up every day trying to figure out where I belonged. My parents forced me to behave and stay grounded while trying to make me the perfect son, only making me angrier with every passing day. I resented them for what they did and for who I became because of them. I felt I'd never find myself again.

I thumbed through documents on my desk at the office, trying my best to stay busy. Otherwise, I would find myself dwelling on just how much of a mess my life had become. It felt like just yesterday, I was finally going to have my way out and escape from my father's shadow forever, but now I was backed into a corner, and a contract dictated I had no option but to stay put.

It was a humiliating experience, but there was a light at the end of the tunnel—I'd met a girl that single-handedly changed my life. Audrey was getting more accustomed to the lifestyle I lived. She dressed differently and spoke more eloquently than she had when we first met, and I was starting to worry about her. I missed her candid charm and the way she always spoke her mind, but now she operated like the same socialite robots that my mother loved to parade around and show off to the crowd of onlookers at the debutante ball.

Every time I brought the subject up, Audrey would shut me down and tell me that she was doing just fine, that it was all part of her master plan to show the world the true nature of Manhattan's elite, but I was starting to feel like she was enjoying herself a little too much. Audrey was getting so accustomed to the luxuries that I could see the look on her face change every time she had to head home to her apartment or return to work down at Greer's, the old bookstore where I'd met her. The girl I was falling for dissipated, and I watched as she turned into another Cece while I tried to figure out what to do.

Ever since my family had joined forces with the Richfields, my life had been a living hell. It was hard enough to have to work alongside my ex-best friend. I was reminded every day that Eric had slept with Cece when Cece and I were still together. It was awful despite his trying desperately to get back in my good graces. I certainly wasn't having any of it, nor did I want any part in whatever he had going on behind the scenes.

Eric was always partying, and occasionally, I had such a terrible day at work that I almost joined him. It wasn't long ago that he was trying to convince me to give up my good-boy ways and return to a life I barely remembered, one that was full of alcohol and one-night stands. It wasn't the kind of life I wanted to lead anymore, and it certainly wouldn't go down well with my family.

Ever since I'd pulled that stunt trying to expose my father's business practices, my parents kept me on a very tight leash, making sure that I kept up their perfect standards and showed my face at all the major events. I remembered the days when they hated to see Audrey on my arm and when the thought of her made my mother's skin crawl, but they were starting to warm up to the idea of her, and I wasn't sure whether that scared me more.

Audrey would deny she was changing until it was time to finish the manuscript she'd been writing about the façade everyone in my life lived behind. I was starting to think she was going to chuck the entire idea to live out her life the way I always feared she would want to—as another socialite wannabe. I knew I had to remind her of the good times and the times when she was only trying to understand why my life had been so hard and why the people who were supposed to care the most about me only ever tried to tear me down. I wished I would've had the answers to those questions a long time ago. If I had, it probably would've kept her from turning out the way she did. I worried there wouldn't be anything I could do to help change her mind when she was too far gone.

She'd been juggling smaller writing jobs across different magazines while she slowly distanced herself from Greer's. I wouldn't be surprised if she left the place behind entirely. I was proud of her for getting her work out there, but the more I saw her succeed, the less I recognized her. I tried to stand by her side and be there for her like I had promised, but the changes were putting a damper on our relationship. I'd returned home for the rest of the day, knowing I was supposed to meet her for lunch, but I just needed a few moments to myself. There was so much about my life that overwhelmed me and so much that I still had yet to process, so it felt good just to collapse onto the chaise lounge in my living room and close my eyes for a while.

I heard the door to my suite open, and Audrey strolled in, looking as beautiful as ever. Her hair was pulled back into a French twist, her lips were a perfect shade of pink, and her ensemble was perfectly ironed. She was barely recognizable as the Audrey she used to be, but I tried to look toward the positive. She was here, she was with me, and I had a lot to be grateful for. I promised myself that I would do everything in my power to remind her that she didn't want to be a part of this world and that if I was given the opportunity, I would've gone running in the other direction a long time ago.

"Hello, Jamie. I was about to head to your office, but I was told that you came home. Are you feeling all right? We can skip lunch if you want," she said. I really wanted to curl up with her, stay in for a little while, and remember what it felt like when we were trying to escape the chaos that surrounded us every day.

"I'll be all right. If we leave now, we can still make lunch. How is your book coming along?" I asked.

I knew it was a touchy subject, but bringing it up was probably the only way that she could see that things had changed. I was tired of hiding my true feelings and pretending that everything was okay when it clearly wasn't. She needed to be jolted back to reality because she couldn't continue living a lie for the rest of her life. She needed to be reminded that the people she saw every day and the people she was spending far too much time with were vindictive, terrible human beings who would throw her under the bus the first chance they got if the situation called for it.

"I've been writing every chance I get. Things have been a little hectic lately, but I have to say that it's coming along. Though I've just landed a small position as a column writer for this upcoming magazine, and I'm really excited about it. I think it may finally be time for me to leave Greer's behind for good," she said, her eyes gleaming, and I tried to force a smile for her.

"Are you sure you want to leave that place behind so soon? It feels like it was just yesterday I was picking you up from there so we could head out for lovely evenings and spend time together. I miss that," I said, and I watched her entire expression change.

"Those were good times, Jamie, but we both have so much going on right now. There's nothing wrong with looking to the future, is there? We were both also dealing with a lot of pain at that time, and we had both lost so much. I'm glad things are finally starting to look up," she said, looking rather sad that I wasn't as excited for her as she wanted me to be.

"I'm happy for you, Audrey. There is no one better suited for the position. Your writing is incredible, and I can't wait to see it in action," I said.

She leaned in to plant a soft kiss on my lips, drawing me up out of my seat so we could head off to lunch together. There were times I felt like I was too hard on her. Maybe she was just going through an adjustment period, and I needed to cut her some slack, but I hated to see the best parts of her disappear.

Even though she seemed to be the same Audrey I knew and loved when she was with me, I'd seen how she interacted with other people when she thought I wasn't looking. It wasn't like her, and I needed her to see that it was time for her to snap out of it. I could tell that she was on edge, and she was dealing with a lot, but there was no reason for her to go through this big change. I didn't want her to turn out like Cece, and I felt sure she wouldn't want that, either, if she had a good, long look in the mirror at the woman she was becoming.

We pulled up to the little French restaurant that had quickly become one of our favorite spots in town. It was the place I'd promised her I'd take her to Paris one day when we both had the chance so she could taste real Parisian food, and I remembered the look of utter gratitude and excitement on her face. Now, it seemed like nothing I did could warrant the same reaction, and I was starting to feel like I was losing her to the luxuries of my life. I thought about all the ways I could approach the conversation. I tried to convince myself that there might be a better time than our lunch together to bring it up, but I just couldn't help myself. The worry was starting to burn a hole in my brain, and if I didn't get it off my chest sooner rather than later, I was surely going to explode.

We sat down at our table in the back, peering over our menus and ordering the same entrées we always got when I reached over the table to squeeze her hand lightly.

"Audrey, I need to talk to you about something, but I don't know how best to bring it up without hurting your feelings," I started, and she looked at me, seeming concerned for what I was about to say next. For a moment, I thought I saw a glimmer of the old Audrey.

"What's bothering you, Jamie?" she asked softly.

"I noticed you've been a little swept up in all the changes you're going through, and you're becoming a person who I barely recognize anymore. I'm sorry that I have to put it that way, but I don't know how else to tell you that you're losing yourself in all of this. I know you say that you had to do this to get the information you need to write your book and that you had to play the part to get close enough, but you're not playing anymore, Audrey. This is who you are now," I said. I watched her get angrier as I spoke.

Her eyes crinkled, and her lips parted slowly as she chose her words carefully. "What are you saying, Jamie? I thought we both agreed that even though these changes were going to be difficult for us, we were going to hang in there because we love each other. Why bring this up when you know it isn't true? I'm never going to be like those girls, Jamie, no matter how I dress or how I behave. I'm still trying to find myself, and I'm barely getting by, but I'm not turning into one of them. I'm just not."

"You haven't seen or acknowledged the way you've been acting over the last few weeks, Audrey, but I've kept a close eye on you. You're starting to act a lot like—"

"Who? Cece? The girl that cheated on you with your best friend? That is who you're comparing me to?" she asked angrily, getting up out of her seat to storm out of the restaurant.

"Audrey, wait!"

"No, I don't have to listen to this right now. Have fun dining by yourself," she said.

She was in a cab before I had the chance to stop her. I hoped there was a chance I got through to her and that she wasn't going to head home and think everything was fine when it wasn't. I didn't want to break the news to her like that, but I had no other choice. If she wasn't careful, she was going to turn into the one thing she'd hated ever since we met. I wasn't going to allow that to happen.

I stayed, finishing up the rest of my meal and paying the bill before I looked down at the clock and noticed I should head back to the office for the meeting I needed to attend. It was another excuse for Eric to weasel his way back into my life, trying to get me to forgive him for all the terrible things he'd done. It wasn't going to be that easy. When I arrived, my assistant came into my office, peeking her head in so she could tell me that my father wanted to see me. I wondered what it could be about as I slammed the file in my hand down on the table and made my way over to the grand double doors of his office. I saw he was alone.

"Sit, son. We need to have a chat," he said, not even bothering to sugar coat how disinterested he looked. I wondered why he couldn't have just passed the message on through my assistant.

"What is it, Father?" I asked, and he looked up at me from behind his glasses, taking them off and pinching the bridge of his nose while he contemplated how to begin.

"I've noticed that you and Eric have been at each other's throats ever since I got him a job here, seeing as his family has just as much stake in the company as we do," he started, and I already knew where this was going.

"And? What's your point, Father?"

"I think it's time that you two work out your differences. It's starting to affect our image, and that is not something that I can stand for anymore. I've already spoken to Eric, and he seems to be trying to get you to forgive him for whatever stupid, childish thing you've both been fighting about. Please, work this out before I have to find a way to do it myself. Just remember, Jamie, women come and go, but the friendships you make at your age stay forever. You won't be able to see that now, but I guarantee you will when you're my age," he said.

I knew he was trying to take a jab at me because I was still seeing Audrey after he'd done everything he could think of to stop me. It was the one thing I told him that he needed to allow me to do. He would rather that than seeing me act out again.

It was hard for me to get through to him because he never could be negotiated with. He always had an agenda. It was usually one that I was against, but I learned my lesson the moment he took everything away from me and reminded me that I was locked in a contract that I couldn't escape. My only option was to continue living out my life under his rules, but now I didn't have the planned escape that I once did.

Mine and Audrey's relationship flourished because she only got involved to expose the wealthy elites for their suspicious and sometimes criminal behavior. I could only hope that she snapped out of it soon. I needed her back. I couldn't do this alone. I couldn't go on knowing that she was going to become another one of them. I walked out of my father's office to see Eric standing there with the biggest grin on his face. He was probably the one that had orchestrated the ordeal, but I had no other option but to bite.

"Join me for a few drinks and a little fun tonight, won't you?" he asked.

I don't have any other choice, do I?

CHAPTER TWO: AUDREY

I was fuming. I couldn't believe he would say something like that to me after everything we'd been through together. I'd shown him time and time again that the only reason I'd worked to get so close was that I saw a story to tell. Was there any truth to what he said? Was I really getting swept up in the luxury of it all?

I tossed my purse and tweed coat onto the bed, another price tag that was going to set me back rent for the month. I heard a knock on my door, and Claire came in. She was wearing an expression of utter concern, and I already knew where the conversation was headed. Not her, too.

"Audrey? Can we talk?" she asked, and I motioned for her to join me on the bed.

She glanced over at the open laptop on my desk and the lukewarm tea I'd forgotten to take to the kitchen before I left for the morning, and when she glanced back at me, I knew she was going to have a hard time telling me how she really felt.

"What is it, Claire?"

"I have to be honest with you because I am your best

friend. Do you have any idea how deep you've gotten in all of this? You eat, sleep, and breathe everything you used to hate about Jamie's world now, and it's terribly hard for me to sit back and watch. I'm sure he probably has seen the same thing, judging from how upset you were storming back in here. You need to have a good look at yourself in the mirror. Your career is taking off, and you're about to have everything you could've ever wanted. I don't want you throwing that away because you got wrapped up in something you can't control. You're different now, Audrey, and I just want my friend back," she said, looking down at the floor like she was afraid of her words.

Hearing it from her made my heart hurt even worse, and I knew I had to have a good, long look at myself. The last thing I wanted was to turn into another Cece. That would be my absolute nightmare. I remembered the night where Cece dragged me into the bathroom, listing off all the things I'd never have and telling me about the person I was never going to become. Part of me wanted to prove her wrong, but I saw now that I'd gone too deep and needed to get out before it was too late.

I glanced back at Claire, who was worried that I was going to blow up at her. I could've sworn she was bracing for it, but instead, I outstretched my arms to hug her, letting down my hair as I tousled it. I didn't need to parade myself around the rich to get an inside look at their lives. They were probably all laughing at me behind my back, anyway. They probably looked down at me for trying to be one of them when I entered their world as someone who hated every single characteristic they possessed. It was time that changed. It was time I remembered who I was. I rested my head on Claire's shoulder, and I could hear her take a sigh of relief.

"So, you're not mad?" she asked.

"I'm not mad. I got a little in over my head, I suppose. I

tried to be someone I'm not, telling myself that I was doing it just for the sake of the story when I was actually falling in the ruse of a life I don't want. The only reason I stuck around for as long as I did is because of Jamie. He's lost so much, and he almost had his way out before his parents snatched it away from him. I was supposed to be the person who would open everyone's eyes to how fake and downright terrible those people are, and instead, I was masquerading around as one of them," I said, realizing that I'd been too hard on Jamie for simply telling me the truth, just as I always asked that he would.

"He's going to thank me for this," she said, with a chuckle.

"Oh no, did he call you?" I asked with a laugh.

"He needed me to rein in the monster," she said, and I shoved her playfully while she headed out of my room, giving me a moment alone.

I walked over to my desk, letting my fingertips brush over the keys that hadn't been used in quite a while. I'd just landed a position that I would've killed to have when I first moved to New York. It was my chance to tell incredible stories without having to sugar coat a thing, and after everything that happened with losing the job opportunity with Cece's mother, I never thought that I would get the chance to move forward and finally come into my own. Though there was still the question of the book and whether or not I was going to continue it. I knew in my heart that it was what needed to be done, and so I opened the draft I'd left when I got a little distracted, finding the words that hadn't flowed so easily in such a long time, and I felt like myself again.

I wrote for the rest of the evening, glancing up at the window above my desk to see that the sun had gone down. I genuinely couldn't remember the last time I'd sat in one place for so long, writing my heart away, trying to tell the stories that mattered to me. It felt incredible, and the only person I wanted to share that feeling with was Jamie. I had no idea where he was, but I decided to give him a call, hoping that he wasn't still too upset about how we left things. The phone rang for what felt like ages, and I could barely hear the voice on the other end of the line over the loud music and shouting in the background. When I was finally able to make it out, I realized it wasn't Jamie who answered the phone at all.

"Jamie?"

"Sorry, lovely. He can't come to the phone right now. He's a little too wasted. Though if you want to come party with us, I'll be happy to text you our location," he said, and I heard my cell phone ping in my ear as the text message came through.

"Eric, is that you?" I asked.

"The one and only. I hope to see you here. Wear something sexy. Jamie told me you two haven't done much of anything lately. If you don't want to start sharing him with someone else, you better get down here," he said, and I couldn't believe him.

"You're lying. There's no way that Jamie would be out partying right now," I said.

"No? Jamie! Come here," he said, and I heard him hand the phone over.

"Audrey, is that you?" Jamie asked.

I didn't know what to say. I couldn't wrap my head around the fact that he was out with Eric, behaving like his old self. This was the part of him that Cece warned me would resurface. "You're one to talk about my behavior when you're out with Eric," I said.

I could hear the large number of people talking over him, which made it difficult to focus on whatever he said next.

"It doesn't matter. I'm coming to get you," I said, hanging up the phone.

I let Claire know where I was heading, slipping into something a bit more appropriate before taking a cab to the club Eric had sent me. My blood boiled at the thought because I knew that whatever Eric was up to, it was certainly no good. It dawned on me that I was so caught up in my own world that I didn't even see what had been happening with Jamie. Eric was back in his life now, and I knew there was bound to be some trouble. I arrived at the club a little later, pushing through the crowd and hoping to catch sight of Jamie. He was in the corner, alone in a booth, mulling over his drinks. Eric was nowhere to be found.

I was shocked to see him disoriented and with absolutely no idea where he was. He was on the verge of being blackout drunk. I needed to get him home, but Eric was living in the same building as him, and I wanted to get him far away from that place. It was bad enough that their families were so close now and that Jamie had much more to worry about than his own parents, but now it seemed like Eric's only goal was to get rid of Jamie for good. Seeing him like that, barely hanging onto what was left of his humanity and downing another lonely drink while everyone else around him appeared to be having such a good time, was all I needed to jolt me back to reality. What had I been doing? How could I have let things get this bad when I knew what these people were capable of? I pushed my way over to him, but right before I could get his attention, someone tapped me on the shoulder.

"Now, this is the last person I'd think to see in a place like this. Are you done playing princess? People see right through you, Audrey. They can sense it from the moment you walk into a room. You don't belong, and you never will. I thought I told you that back at the Forrest house," Cece said, looking as gorgeous as ever with a drink in her hand.

"I have nothing to say to you, Cece. I'm going to get Jamie out of here, and he's going to be furious when he eventually snaps out of this phase he's in. I don't know what you and Eric are up to, but I can already tell you that Jamie is going to see right through you both. He doesn't hang around vapid, shallow bitches," I said, and she looked taken aback. Then, I watched her lips turn up into a smile.

"Oh, he always has, honey. It seems that's exactly the kind of person you want to be, but I have no business prying. Jamie has said how disappointed he's been in your behavior and how much he misses the old you, but he'll soon come to his senses and realize that you two were never going to last. You should just give it up while you can," she said.

I scoffed, pushing past her to get to Jamie. I didn't want to hear another word. I didn't want her telling me that I didn't belong in her world when I was sure that I didn't want any part in it, anyway. I had a momentary lapse in judgment, but I had to remember that the people around me weren't my friends. Some of them may have taken pity on me, but they only interacted with me because they either felt bad or thought they could use me for personal gain. I was not going to have any part in that anymore. I was going to get back to doing what I loved. When the time came, I'd expose them for who they really were.

I rushed over to Jamie, watching his eyes widen when he finally realized that it was me.

"Audrey? What are you doing here?" he asked, confused.

"I'm here to get you out of here, Jamie. You don't belong in a place like this, and if my judgment is right, Eric only brought you here so he could get you wasted enough to further his agenda. I'm not going to let him do that. Let's go," I said, helping him up.

He struggled to stand, and I helped him out to the front of the building. His car was absolutely nowhere to be found. I held him up, feeling the weight of his body weigh me down while I tried my best to hail a cab. I eventually got one. I asked the driver to help him inside, breathing a sigh of relief that I got him out of there before something bad happened.

"My friend has had a little too much to drink. Thank you, sir," I said to the cab driver, giving him my home address as we took off into the night.

I tried to jolt Jamie awake, but he was having a hard time keeping his eyes open. I knew that something else had to be going on. There is no way he managed to get so much alcohol in him that he couldn't even function. The man drank more whiskey than water. I felt the pit in my stomach grow heavy at the thought that something terrible must've been going on. I knew that Eric was a terrible person, as was Cece, but I didn't think they were capable of trying to hurt Jamie for their own personal gain. Deep down, I was sure that they would never want to physically harm him. They may inconvenience him or take away the things he cared about the most, but there was no way I could believe he was in any real danger.

The taxi pulled up outside the small townhouse I shared with Claire, and I helped Jamie up the stairs, getting him through the front door, where he collapsed onto my couch. Claire stared at him blankly, trying to figure out why I would've brought him here. I knew I had a lot of explaining to do. She and I ventured off into the kitchen, where I filled the kettle and placed it on the stove, peering into the living room every few minutes to make sure that Jamie was doing all right. He was knocked out completely now, and his breathing slowed into a calm rhythm. I was glad that he was out of harm's way for the time being.

"That conversation of yours must've gotten quite interesting for him to be so out of it now," Claire said, and I shook my head.

"We didn't even get the chance to talk. I walked in on him sitting in the back of the bar, downing drink after drink and looking completely out of it. I don't know how he ended up in a place like that. Since I've known him, he never once stepped foot into a club that wasn't a familial obligation or work celebration of some kind. He always held his own very well, and I've never seen him like this. I've been so caught up in my own drama that I didn't even realize something terrible could still be going on. Now, I have no idea what to do," I explained to Claire.

"And you're sure this behavior is completely new to him? You did tell me that he was quite the partier before you two met. Maybe he just went off the deep end a little bit. He's been dealing with a lot, as well, ever since he's been boxed into following his parents' rules," Claire said.

"That may be so, but he doesn't seem like he's having much of a good time, does he? I don't have a very good feeling, Claire. What was even weirder was that he was there with Eric. He hates Eric's guts and everything that he's about. Just because he has to see him at the office every day doesn't mean that he's going to willingly go out with him at night," I said, shaking my head. The kettle started to whistle as I pulled it off of the stove.

"He may not have wanted to go, but maybe his father had something to do with this. From what you've told me, that man is shadier than even I expected. I've seen a lot of men do terrible things, some who I've had to represent in court. Men like Mr. Forrest always seem to have an agenda. They're not happy until everyone around them completely fears their existence, and they seem to want to take whatever they can get from whoever they want. They don't believe in consequences. It's time you get your investigative skills out.

There may be more to the story than you originally thought," Claire said, and I couldn't agree more.

I knew there were businessmen who prided themselves on breaking the law and feeling like they were invincible, and something about seeing what happened to Jamie made me believe that there were bigger problems in play. I'd have to ask him about it all when he woke up because he was out cold right now. I was more worried than I had been since he asked to take me to his parents' house, where they held a pretty wild intervention.

I wondered how greedy of a man Theodore Forrest really was, because judging from what I'd seen, he would do anything to fill his pockets and live out a lavish lifestyle. He was always hungry for the next big business deal, tearing down anyone that got in his way. I could only hope that Jamie wasn't one of Mr. Forrest's setbacks, and I wanted to believe that no matter how terrible their relationship was, he would never give up on Jamie. I knew I never would.

CHAPTER THREE: JAMIE

Where the hell was I? What happened to me?
My eyelids fluttered open to reveal a
normal-looking living room. I reached to the
back of my head to feel a terrible headache start to form. I
tried to get up, but any sudden movements immediately
made me feel like I wanted to vomit. I had no recollection of
what happened the night prior after I agreed to go with Eric
out to the club. I only wanted to get him off my back and
make sure that he knew I wasn't in the market for another
best friend but that I would try to keep things civil because
we were working together. It seemed that he had other plans
for me.

I glanced down at my wristwatch to see the time, realizing that I had already missed an important work meeting. I
knew my father was going to have my head when I saw him
again. This was probably exactly what Eric wanted—to show
my father that I was unfit to lead the position I'm in. The
man couldn't take working a position under me, and he was
doing everything in his power to undermine my success. It
didn't surprise me that Eric would try to get me down, but

what did shock me was that I fell directly into his trap. I began to worry that I might have done something terrible while I was wasted, especially because Audrey and I had left things in a terrible place, but I had no right to act out.

I began to worry that I was in another girl's apartment and had passed out on the couch, but I realized I was still fully dressed. That was certainly a good sign. I heard pots clanking in the kitchen, and I groaned as I saw someone approach me. When I fully came to, I realized it was Audrey.

"Am I glad to see you," I said.

She leaned down to kiss me. It felt so nice to feel her soft lips on mine, and there was something different about her. She looked like herself again, the beautiful wide-eyed girl with every dream imaginable.

"It's good to have you back, too, Jamie," she said with a smile.

"Did I wake up in an alternate universe where you're finally yourself again?" I asked, hearing my voice crack, and she handed me a glass of water.

"No, but I did knock some sense into her while you were out partying with your mortal enemy," Claire said from the kitchen. I could smell the breakfast she'd been preparing, and while I was sure it was perfectly exquisite, any sign of food made my stomach turn.

"I'm so sorry that you had to put up with me behaving like another Cece. I had no idea how bad it had gotten until I saw how they were treating you at the club. You were there, in the back alone, and Eric was nowhere to be found. You could barely string two words together, Jamie. I've never seen you like that before," she said, and that shocked me.

"I've never been like that before, nor have I ever had a hangover this bad. It doesn't make any sense. My father told me that I needed to start mending fences with Eric because the animosity between us was going to be bad for business, but I didn't think that Eric would leave me there like that unless he has a completely different idea of how things are going to go than I do," I said, realizing that Eric must've had an ulterior motive that required me to be out of it for a little while.

"Why would he do this to you?" Audrey asked.

I saw the genuine concern on her face. I was just glad that she was looking like herself again. She no longer seemed to be pretending to be a socialite, and I could tell that there was a fire lit inside of her yet again.

"He probably wanted to impress the board at the meeting we were both supposed to head today. Maybe he thought that if he could get me out of the way, he could prove to my father that my priorities were elsewhere," I said, my blood boiling at the very thought.

"Well, is there still time? Could you make it if we left right now?" she asked, and I knew she was trying everything she could to help, but it was going to be no use.

"The meeting has been over for hours, and I know I'm going to have to face the music once I get back to the office, but I suppose I had it coming. I should've known better than to trust Eric, even for a moment, knowing how terrible he's been to me in the past. Did you see anything else suspicious at the club?" I asked her, hoping she could paint a better picture than I could because my memories were all fuzzy.

"I don't know if I can refer to it as suspicious, but Cece was there. She seemed to be keeping an eye on you, but for what reason, I wasn't sure. She had a few choice words to share, all the more to bring me back to reality, but I'm glad that I'm back on track. I started writing again, and I see now that these people are never going to change. They deserve to be written about, the same way that they live their lives exploiting the people that get in their way," she said, and it

was like music to my ears to hear that she was back at
it again.

"I'm so glad to hear that, Audrey. You have no idea how
worried I was about you," I said, watching her lean in for
another kiss.

"Trust me, Jamie, after I saw the way you were last night,
I can imagine you were just as worried as I was then. We're
going to get to the bottom of this, just like I promised we
would. I won't let the luxuries of your world entice me any
longer. I know where my priorities are now, and even though
I'm well on my way to building a career for myself, that
doesn't mean that I'm going to lose who I am in the process,"
she said.

"Thank God for that," I said, kissing her lightly as Claire
brought over a lovely omelet and toast. I just couldn't
stomach it.

"What? It's not that bad," she said, looking at my facial
expression.

"No, it's just that I'm a little nauseous. Uh, Audrey.
Where's your bathroom?" I asked.

She pointed to the ensuite in her bedroom, where I spent
the next hour vomiting my guts out. Audrey spent the day
nursing me back to health, making sure that I had everything I needed to feel better. It was nice to finally curl up
with her and pretend that my life wasn't a chaotic mess. She
filled me in on all the writing she'd been doing and how
excited she was to start her new position having her very own
column in a magazine. This time, I was sure she wasn't
blinded by the allure of the socialite lifestyle. This time, she
wasn't doing these things to impress people. She was
genuinely happy that she got the opportunity. I was proud of
her, and I wanted her to know just how proud I was. She
had been the only thing keeping me going for a very long
time, and there was a point where I truly thought I was

going to lose her for good, but now I could see that we were in this together.

I understood that my life was hanging on by a thread at this point. I had to figure out what Eric was up to before he did something that could undermine the entire family business. Since I'd been forced to stay, I had to do what I could to protect it, especially if there was even the slightest chance that my father was going to turn it over to me one day. I hoped my father didn't make a grave mistake by letting the Richfields in on a company that has been strictly in the Forrest name since it was founded. I was so ready to leave, so ready to break out on my own that I didn't even consider the lengths my father would go to convince me to stay. Now, I could see that I still had a lot of learning to do. The only way I was going to ever find my footing on my own would be to show everyone around me that I was the only one holding the business together.

I wouldn't have been surprised if the Richfields had been planning something like this all along because that was the kind of people they were. Eric had always bragged about how his father never cared about what he had to do to get ahead, but I'd heard rumors that he got his start borrowing some money from the kind of people none of us wanted to mess with. I could only hope that they didn't rope my father into something like that because it would be the end of Forrest Industries as we knew it. I wasn't going to allow Eric to take the business away from me the way he stole Cece out of my arms. The more I dwelled on the possibility that my entire life was going to go up in flames very soon, the sicker I felt.

Audrey had fallen asleep next to me, and it was nice to see her so peaceful. I wished I could've holed up in her apartment, but I knew that the more I sat around, the more time I was going to give Eric to solidify his place in the company, and I certainly wasn't going to allow that to happen. I tried to get up from the couch without waking her, but the moment I moved, she began to stir.

"Leaving so soon?" she asked, pulling me back down so she could plant another kiss on my lips, and I wanted to hold her right there in my arms for the rest of the evening.

"I wish I didn't have to go, but I have to smooth things over with my father, though I would rather do just about anything else. I have to get to the bottom of what's really going on here because if my family's company is in danger, I have to do something about it. Maybe if I manage to stop whatever the Richfields have planned, my father will finally let me go," I said, and she smiled.

"I'll be here if you need anything. I'll continue trying to weasel my way back into your world, but this time, I won't allow myself to get caught up in it, and if for some reason I do, I know I have you and Claire to bring me back down to earth," she said. I planted a kiss on her forehead.

"I don't know what I would do without you, Audrey. Once this is all over, and we can finally relax again, I'll be sure to whisk you away to Paris so you can finally try some real French cuisine. That was our plan, remember?" I asked.

"How could I forget?" she replied, kissing me softly as I got ready to leave.

I bid her goodbye, taking the first cab back home. I hoped things weren't going to be too difficult for me to deal with when I faced my father.

WHEN I ARRIVED BACK AT my SUITE, IT WAS EMPTy AND freshly cleaned with towels laid out on the bed. It felt lifeless, and I wanted nothing more than to forget about it entirely and head back to Audrey's apartment downtown. I realized it was the first place I'd genuinely felt happy in a while. I never had anyone be there for me the way that Audrey was before, and she made me feel like there was still hope after all. She knew I wasn't going to stand for whatever Eric had planned, and the only way I was going to get enough information on him would be to get close to him the way my father had wanted me to. Only now, I was going to be on high alert for any suspicious behavior. If Eric was already working to make me look terrible to the board, I could only imagine he had other things planned, as well.

There was no shortage of boring nights when he was around because he always managed to party until the wee hours of the morning and still show up for work the next day. I used to think it was a talent of his, but now I saw he just liked putting on a show. I decided that the best bet would be to play him for a fool. I would invite him down to the bar nestled into the back of the lobby so that we could have a real chat about why he'd been so adamant on getting in my good books ever since our fathers joined forces. I dialed his number, waiting patiently as it rang, and it wasn't long before he answered.

"Jamie! Missed you at the meeting this morning, man. Your father was absolutely furious, but don't worry, I covered for you as best as I could. Though he's probably going to have a talk with you soon enough," he said. I wished I could've given him another punch straight to the lip, but I had to calm my rage and keep things good between us.

"I don't know, man. I probably drank a little too much last night, but at least no one has to know about that, right? After all, you did leave me there to get even more wasted," I said, trying to fish for a bit of information on his where-abouts after he left me.

"You were wasted, and I got caught up trying to get in this girl's pants. Nothing has really changed, Jamie. You'll see that soon enough. What is this really about? I'm sure you're not calling because you want to head back out on the town, or do you?" he asked.

"I think you should come by the bar. I'd like to have a chat with you in person," I said, and he agreed.

What was he up to, and who was he trying to sell me out to? I got a text message from Eric soon after, telling me that he was in the lobby. I hurried downstairs. I still felt exhausted from waking up in a daze, but I had to keep my head on straight. I hung around the elevator for a moment, watching him type furiously away at the screen on his phone, and I could only wonder what would've gotten him so upset. If I could get a hold of his phone, maybe I could get answers that I would otherwise have to wait much longer to find. He was doing everything he could to prove to everyone that I was unfit to run my father's company or even work at it, and it was time he got a taste of his own medicine. I waved to him just as he spotted me approaching.

"Let's drink, shall we? I'm surprised you're still standing after all the shots you put away last night," he said, leading me into the bar.

"As you said, Eric, some things never change," I replied. I watched that incessant grin appear on his face while we both took our seats, ordering a variety of different concoctions to try.

"You know how you said no one had to know about your little outing last night?" Eric asked, and my heart immediately sank into my stomach. He handed me his phone, showing me that my face was once again plastered across every online tabloid magazine there was.

"So, this is what you wanted," I said, taking the phone into my hands.

"What do you mean?" he asked, trying to play dumb with me.

"Do you really think that you're going to win my father

over by getting me out of the picture, Eric? What is that going to accomplish?" I asked.

"I wasn't trying to do anything of the sort, man. If they caught wind of what was going down at the club, that's because you were back to your old self for the night. If you ask me, there's nothing really wrong with that, is there? You needed a night off to blow off some steam and hang out with your best friend, and your father is going to understand that. After all, you are his son, and he did everything he could think of to get you to stay, even when you were the one trying to betray him," he said, downing an entire glass of scotch.

"You had a hand in making sure that never happened, so I'm sure he must be grateful to you for that," I scoffed.

"I was just trying to protect you. Once that story of yours hit the shelves, you were going to be a laughing stock amongst every single corporation in the country. They don't care about startup advice and taking down the big fish, Jamie. They want to be one of them. You already have that, and you're doing everything you can to throw it away. I still can't figure out why," Eric said.

"I didn't want this life, Eric. It was handed to me on a silver platter, and I grew tired of having everything handed to me. For once, I wanted to break out on my own and do something that was entirely my own, but you and everyone else in my life made sure that was never going to happen. So, forgive me if I'm a little upset that after everything you've done to me, you would try to make my life that much harder," I said.

I watched his expression soften. I saw a glimmer of who he used to be, and just like that, I was left feeling like I could possibly get under his skin again. Maybe I could make him believe I was going to be his best friend again, the one he thought he lost so long ago.

"It doesn't have to be this way, Jamie. You and I could do incredible things together if we just manage to get over this rough patch. Don't you see that?" he asked, and I nodded.

"I suppose there may be some truth to that. I used to enjoy having you around before you turned into a narcissistic asshole," I said teasingly.

"I was always a narcissistic asshole, but so were you, and that's why you never noticed."

"If I agree to let bygones be bygones, you have to promise to stop trying to change me. It's going to take me some time to adjust to the idea of having you back, much less revisiting my old self. Clearly, I'm out of practice," I said, and he laughed.

"Don't worry about it, Jamie. I have your back, and together we're going to make both of our fathers proud," he said.

I realized that could've very well been what it was about. Just like me, Eric had been vying for his father to recognize the work he's done over the years, but it was never good enough. That very fact was the one thing that brought us together in the first place, and it might be the one thing I could use against him when I beat him at his own game.

Watch your back, Eric. You have no idea what's going to happen now that I know you're here to wreak havoc.

CHAPTER FOUR: AUDREY

I was still so worried about Jamie. He left feeling fine, but now I was scared that Eric was going to get him wrapped up in something that would destroy his career forever. I spent the evening looking at all the paparazzi photos of him before I rescued him from the club, and he looked completely out of it. I could only imagine what his father was going to say, and I worried that this might be the last straw before his father started to look into other disciplinary measures.

I closed my laptop screen, unable to look at those photos any longer. I sat on the edge of my bed, trying to figure out how I was going to get close enough to people he knew to continue writing my book and help him figure out what was really going on. My mind immediately went to Cece, and I knew that she was probably much more in the loop than anyone else in Eric's circle. There was nothing I could do to get her to take me seriously, especially now that she'd let me know that she could see right through my attempts at fitting in.

I heard my phone ping with an email, and I ran through

it to see it was a request for a meeting the following day with the Editor-in-Chief of the magazine that hired me to write a column. They wanted a fresh look at New York life, and I knew that I could provide that and more. They wanted to discuss how things were going to proceed, what I would be writing about, and how important it would be for me to get out on the town and do something worth writing about.

I wondered if these larger magazine editors all knew each other. In a place like Manhattan, I wouldn't be surprised if they did. I realized that the one way I could get to Cece was through her mother. If her mother were to see that I was hired by someone she knew after Cece begged her to fire me, it was bound to get a reaction out of her. It may even make her want to get close to me and keep an eye on me the same way she was keeping an eye on Jamie. This might be what I needed to get back in and solidify myself as a part of their crowd long enough for them to share their secrets. I was going to have to snoop, ask the right questions, and be ready to face the consequences if things went wrong, but it was all worth a shot. I had a way in now. I just had to hope that it was going to work.

I spent the rest of the afternoon writing, trying to turn in a bit earlier because I knew that I would have to be up bright and early for my meeting. I decided to give Jamie a call to check in on how he was doing and make sure that his little run-in with Eric didn't leave him too upset.

"Audrey," he said, sounding rather tired himself.

"How are you? How did things go tonight?" I asked, hoping that he was alone. He sounded like he was tucked in bed, as well.

"I'm all right. I miss you quite a lot. It seems that Eric took the bait, and he's well on his way to believing that we're going to be friends again. At least this way I can find out what he's up to, but he's probably going to drag me to a few more parties along the way. I hope you will attend with me," he said, and I smiled.

"Well, someone's going to have to drag you home when you've had a bit too much to drink, huh?" I teased.

"My hero. Are you heading to bed now?" he asked.

"Yes, I have to meet with the Editor-in-Chief of Blank Page first thing tomorrow. I'm excited yet incredibly nervous to see how my column is going to go," I said, and I could hear the excitement on the other end of the line, reminding me that Jamie had been my biggest supporter all along, even when I couldn't see it for myself.

"I'm so happy for you, Audrey. I know after what happened a few months ago, things have been hectic, especially because you lost every opportunity you had. I'm so proud of you for making your own way, and I'm sure the column is going to be amazing. You'll also finally have an office space of your own, so you won't be waking Claire up in the middle of the night anymore," he teased.

"Oh, she likes it. Though it would be nice to have a space of my own, and I'm probably going to get a cubicle at best. Let's not get ahead of ourselves. I was thinking, do you know if Cece's mother knows the Editor-in-Chief of Blank Page? I know that you have the Eric front completely under control, but I was thinking about how I could get Cece's attention, so I could help figure out what she's up to, as well. Besides, I'm going to need more material if I'm going to be writing a column twice a week for the online publication and once a month for the print version."

"Yes, I do believe they do know each other. That's going to be quite the mission for you, though. Are you sure you're up for it? We both know how it nearly went down last time you tried to get involved with her," he said, warning me, but this time I had my head on straight.

"Don't worry about me, Jamie. I know where my priorities are, and I know now what I need to be looking out for. I'm not going to let any of them get in my head again, and they're certainly not going to be miraculously convinced that I'm a part of their world when they know good and well where I come from. I just want to find out what makes Cece tick. It would come in handy when we have to eventually corner them both and find out what they're up to," I said.

"It's a good idea and a wonderful place to start, but I'm going to keep a close eye on you to make sure that none of this overwhelms you. Deal?"

"Deal," I responded, smiling even though I knew he couldn't see me.

"If you're going to be close tomorrow, stop by after the meeting. I'd love to see you before I have to head to the office and face my father. A little kiss for moral support?" he asked teasingly.

"I will be there. Sleep well, Jamie."

"You too, Audrey."

It felt so good to go to sleep feeling calm for once. I curled up underneath the covers, filled with determination, much like I had felt when I first met Jamie. I took the first few steps to start establishing a career for myself back then, and now I was about to start working at my dream job, having the chance to write about the things that mattered to me. I knew that was going to bring an entirely new list of obstacles to overcome with it, but I was ready for them all. I knew I had a lot to learn about what being a columnist was actually like, but I was passionate, and I had a voice I wanted to share with the world. It would also be nice to have a place to work on my book without the distractions that were clouding my mind every second of every day. As much as I cared about Jamie, and as much as I wanted to do everything I could to help him get to the bottom of what was going on, I couldn't help but feel a bit overwhelmed by the entire situation sometimes. I knew I was going to have to find a balance eventually.

I can't keep juggling both worlds, finding that one always takes priority over the other. I'm going to have to find a way to coexist with the people I don't like because I have a feeling that once I take this job, I'm going to be seeing a lot more of them than I would like. Though I believe this time, I'm going to be ready for it.

CHAPTER FIVE: JAMIE

I woke up to the incessant ringing of my cell phone, and I reached over to answer it groggily, not even bothering to look at the number on the screen.

"Hello, son. I know you don't have to be in the office for a few hours, but just know that we're going to have to talk about your partying problem. I was going to ask you to take charge of the meeting today, but seeing as you've been so busy getting wasted, I'm going to hand that opportunity over to your dear friend. When you decide to start getting your act together, we can talk about you taking up more responsibility here, but until then, you're just going to have to prove to me that you're capable," my father said. I truly wasn't in the mood to deal with him.

"Listen, Father. I've been working my ass off for the better part of the last three years, and I have a lot to show for it, but you chose to ignore it. Need I remind you that I wanted out of the family business? I wanted to move on, but you did everything in your power to keep me right where I am. That was a judgment call you made, and you're going to have to live with it. As for Eric, he was the one that took me to that club, luring me into his old ways on the premise that we were somehow going to become friends again, just like you wanted. Look how that turned out. You can either allow me to focus on work or focus on my friendship. The choice is yours," I said to him, not even bothering to sugar coat how ridiculous his demands had been lately. He was the one that asked me to return to Eric and wave the white flag so that we could set aside our differences. He had no one else to blame for how that turned out.

"We'll talk more about this. Please, just try to stay out of trouble until then," he requested before he hung up the phone, not leaving me much room to answer.

I sighed. It certainly wasn't the way I wanted to start my morning. I was looking forward to seeing Audrey after she'd had her first meeting at Blank Page. After everything that happened and her finding me at the club wasted out of my mind, I was glad that I started to see the old her start to emerge again. I could only hope that with her trying to get close to Cece, she managed to hold her own, not allowing the allure of it all to overwhelm her again. She seemed to finally have her priorities in order and seemed to understand there wasn't anything glamorous about this life. At best, it was chaotic. I thought there wasn't any real danger, but I was starting to think that maybe I'd been wrong about that, as well.

There was something about Eric's behavior that was rubbing me the wrong way, and I found myself thinking about it the entire morning. He knew a lot more than he was letting on. I was well aware that he was a shady man, but I never understood how bad it was until I saw him attend the intervention at my parents' house, where he assisted them in taking my sole business venture away from me. He'd looked like he'd gotten everything he wanted that night, and I still couldn't figure out why that was.

I wanted nothing more than to lock him in a room and get the answers I needed out of him, but I knew that was never going to work. Once I let him out, he was going to run crying wolf to my father as well as his, leaving them both to make the decision to let me go. My father hadn't threatened that he was going to cut me out of the business because he knew what the contract entailed, but that didn't mean he wasn't going to make it incredibly hard for me to succeed if I didn't get my act together the way he wanted.

I wished I could've gone back to sleep, pretending that everything going on in my life was just another nightmare that I was going to be able to wake up from, but I knew I was never going to get that opportunity. I had to get up, head straight for the shower, throw on a ridiculously expensive suit, and make a bunch of risky financial decisions that could potentially ruin my father's company. He trusted my judgment, even if he could never come right out and say it.

I promised myself that when I was at the office, I would keep a closer eye on Eric. If his behavior told me anything, it was that I needed to start digging a little deeper to find the answers I'd been looking for. I was tired of feeling like I was running in circles and like the truth kept escaping from me at the very last second, but at least I could rest assured there was someone else out there helping me from the other angle —the woman that Eric had abandoned our friendship for, Cecilia.

She had been out of my hair for quite a while, and I was starting to think that she might have a monogamous bone in her body. I had a feeling that at the first sign that Eric was starting to lose interest in her, though, she was going to come running back to me, hoping that I'd entertain her after everything that she'd done. I didn't think I'd ever find it in my heart to forgive her, and I knew that my heart belonged to someone else now. Audrey had truly changed me. In such a short amount of time, she had become more important to me than anyone else in my life. I wanted to protect her at all costs and keep her out of the terribly disorderly life I lived, but she always insisted in helping me, no matter how high the stakes were. That was something I always admired about her, and I promised myself that I wouldn't let myself slip because I didn't want to leave her to pick up all the pieces.

I straightened my tie and ran a brush through my hair while I glanced at my reflection in the mirror. There were bags under my eyes from the sleepless nights I'd had over the past week, but I was starting to feel a bit better, knowing that I had something to fixate on.

You're not perfect, Eric, and there will come a time where you do slip up. I will be there to witness it all, and I'll finally be one step closer to understanding what you really want with Forrest Industries.

I WAS ON MY WAY DOWN TO THE LOBBY WHEN I HEARD A familiar voice coming from the concierge's desk. I looked over behind the wall to see Eric standing there, but he wasn't asking to meet me. He was waiting for someone else that lived in the building. I decided to hang back and try to figure out what he could be up to when we were both supposed to be at work soon. I already texted Audrey, letting her know that we could meet in the middle at a local coffee shop instead of having her travel in the opposite direction just to see me, and she agreed. I didn't have long before she would wonder where I was, but I couldn't rest without knowing who Eric was here to see, especially if we were living under the same room. I stayed out of sight, trying to make sure I didn't make eye contact with any of the staff because they were bound to come up to me, asking if I needed assistance.

I watched as Eric met with a man that came in from the revolving door leading into our building. Eric acknowledged him straight away, but I had absolutely no idea who he was. I watched them walk off together, heading over to the other wall of elevators across from me, and I watched the elevator and the little neon number of the counter tick above. They got in together, and I stood there to see which floor they got off at so that I could do a bit of snooping on my own if need be—floor eleven.

I wondered who could be staying there and what they wanted with Eric. I tried to remember every detail of that man's face, just in case I had to dig a bit on my own later. I had to focus on keeping Eric distracted and behaving exactly how he would expect I would. The last thing I needed was for him to start suspecting anything.

I called for my car to be brought around, and I was well on my way to the coffee shop, pulling up in front of it right as Audrey entered. I tapped her lightly on the shoulder, and she turned around with the biggest grin on her face. I hadn't seen her smile like that in such a long time, and it warmed my heart.

"I take it the meeting went well," I said, and she nodded.

We walked inside the little coffee shop, ordered two drinks, and took our seats while we waited. It felt good to be away from all the worries and distractions, even if it was just for a little while. I genuinely wanted to hear about how the girl I was falling for was starting to live out the dreams she'd been after since she first arrived in Manhattan. She approached this like herself, so determined and excited, and I couldn't help but want to share in that with her.

"The meeting went incredibly. My new boss's name is Victoria, and she's going to be keeping a close eye on me to see how my first columns do when they go up online. I have a lot of work to do, but for the first time in a while, I'm incredibly excited. Also, she's inviting me to the magazine launch party, which I hear is going to be a major event where a bunch of other magazines are going to be invited. That means that Cece is probably going to be there, and she's not going to expect to see me," she said, sipping lightly on her coffee.

"I'm so happy for you, Audrey. Please, let me take you out this afternoon to pick out something nice to wear," I offered, wanting to celebrate her because this truly was a big milestone for her.

"No, Jamie. I could never ask you to do that for me."

"Please, I want to. It's such a big occasion for you, and I want to do something nice to celebrate," I said, and she smiled.

"You can do more than enough by accompanying me to the party," she said, and I chuckled.

"All right, it's settled. We'll get complimentary ensembles then."

She nodded, giving in because she knew I was going to keep pressing her. She and I both enjoyed the calm, quiet morning before we'd have to head back to our busy lives, hopefully meeting later that day so I could get her something lovely to wear, something she was going to look at sometime in the future and remember these moments.

"Audrey, I have to tell you something. I saw Eric at my building today. He was meeting with a man that was staying there, and they got off on the eleventh floor. I don't know who he is or what that's about, but Eric is usually at the office much earlier than I am, and he skipped out on that to meet with this guy. Something tells me that he's planning something big or he's involved in something terrible, but I have yet to figure it out. I know this is asking a lot, but if you do manage to get Cece in an answering mood, would you mind scoping her out to see if she might know something?" I asked, feeling terrible that I even had to ask, knowing this was my mess that I needed to deal with.

"Of course, Jamie. I'll be sure to do just that, and this time she's going to have to give me something better than, 'You don't belong here,' because for the first time ever, I'm finally making my way on my own," she said, and I leaned in to kiss her, feeling her soft lips press into mine.

I embraced her before we both took off in separate directions, and I got into the back of my town car, counting down the minutes until I could see her again. I noticed that she had an effect on me, something I never quite felt when I was with Cece. It was the genuine kind of compassion that made being around her so enjoyable, and I didn't want that to ever go away. I was so glad I had her by my side through all of this because I was sure I would have crumbled under the pressure of everything I was dealing with by now.

It was all far too much for me to handle. I felt like I took a backseat, watching the events play out before me while I could do nothing to stop them. I was well aware that I had more control than I may have realized, though. If I did find out that Eric was trying to do something to sabotage Forrest Industries in some way, I was sure my father would side with me in trying to get rid of the threat, especially if Eric and his father were out making promises they could not keep. I tried to imagine how their conversation went, who that man was that he mysteriously led up to the eleventh floor, and what they were planning on doing. It scared me to know that Eric was trying to assume power and trying to strip me of my own because I thought that if he managed to line up enough cavalry, he would be able to do it.

My father was completely blinded by Eric's charm, asking me to get along with him because there was a part of him that wished I would've acted like he did. Eric was charming, charismatic, and everything I was not whenever I was around my father's board members. I got straight to the point, never sugar-coating anything, and that was why I was so good at my job. No matter how much my father tried, he just couldn't deny that, but he would find any reason to criticize me. I wondered if he had any doubts or regrets about signing the papers that joined Forrest Industries with the Richfields because lately, all I saw behind his tired eyes was worry. He didn't seem as on top of things as he usually was, and I worried that they were starting to get to him just as much as they were trying to get to me.

I arrived at my office, and my assistant filled me in on the tasks and meetings I had for the day, asking if I would like for her to get me anything. I politely declined, waiting for her to close the door behind me. I looked out through the glass into Eric's office to see that he was just nowhere to be found. Was he still with that man? The meeting was starting soon, and Eric didn't seem like the type to miss these things.

I went through my calendar, and the thought occurred to me that I could give him a call. It would be a good idea to ruffle his feathers the same way he was trying to do to me. I could get him to think that I was trying to take his position the same way he's been trying to get rid of mine since he first stepped through the front door. I dialed his number, waiting patiently while it rang.

"Can't talk now, Jamie. I'm in the middle of something," he said as soon as he picked up.

"Well, you're probably going to have to get out of it because the meeting is starting soon, and Father said he was looking forward to you heading the schedule today," I lied.

"You're just going to have to handle this one without me, Jamie. I wish I could explain, but unfortunately, this is going to have to wait for another time," he said, and I smiled. I could hear the apprehension in his voice, and he didn't seem to be too amused by my comment.

"Suit yourself," I said, storming into the conference room with my file in hand, ready to show everyone there that I meant business.

I was going to take as much advantage of Eric's absence as I could. The mere fact that he chose the meeting with that man over the one at work meant that he had to be hiding something. I still didn't have many answers, but at least I knew where his priorities were. Right now, I was going to count that as a win. I was going to capture the attention of everyone in the room and show my father that one of us came to work today. It was about time.

CHAPTER SIX: AUDREY

I t's finally Monday morning, my first real day of work at Blank Page. I've never been this scared to mess anything up in my entire life. I wish I could go back to the confident feeling that was coursing through me when I had my first preliminary meeting. Now, I was going to have to start searching for the kind of stories people would want to read, but at least I had a place to start this time. I may not get my book out there right now, but that doesn't mean I can't start shedding a little light on the people that have made a truly big impact on me since I've become a part of Jamie's life.

I packed my bag, gathered my laptop, notebook, and everything I needed to take with me, excited to have a space to call my own where I could start writing stories that were going to resonate with people and that people would be able to learn from the same way I did. It was still my test run, and I had to be careful with the topics I chose because if they weren't well-received, I could see Victoria taking the first opportunity to fire me. She wasn't the kindest person I'd ever met, but she still was the one that invited me to the launch party. Knowing how high of a position she had, she didn't have to do that. It wasn't a company-wide event, and I was glad that I had the opportunity to attend. In the corner of my room, I spotted the lovely Vivienne Westwood box sitting near my bed, which contained the dress Jamie and I had picked out together for the event. Every time I looked at it, I was overcome with joy, excited to finally see myself in a dress that gorgeous.

I knew I still had quite a bit of time to start thinking about that because the launch party wasn't until Friday evening, but I had to have my first column ready to hit the site in two days. I had already drafted a few pieces, making sure to pull out all the stops, edit them heavily, and make sure they were the best they could possibly be before Victoria chose which one to run. I had a lot of material to write about because I'd been living such a complicated life, and Victoria's main message was that she wanted other women to be able to relate to what I was writing about, telling me that it was one of the reasons she had chosen me. I was more than grateful for the opportunity because at least this time, it wasn't relying on the praise from a raging bitch like Cece. I still couldn't believe that after all the work I had done to write that piece for her mother's magazine, she pulled it at the last minute because I got too close to Jamie than she liked.

I still didn't know why she cared so much if she spent all of her time wrapped up in Eric's arms. Unless there was still trouble in paradise. I knew they spent a lot of time together, and I was going to have to use that to my advantage when I eventually grilled her the way she'd done to me in the past. I was sure she would not like it, and that was exactly what I was counting on. I took one last look at myself in my bathroom mirror before I decided it was time to go. Claire was getting ready for work, as well, and it was probably the first time that we'd both been so dolled up so early in the morning.

"Well, you look like you're heading to a law firm to handle a case that's far too big for you to handle," Claire said, teasing me about my smart suit.

"I'm sure that's you. Good luck today, Claire. You're going to do great," I said, giving her a good-luck hug before we both hurried out the front door, hailing separate cabs and taking off in different directions.

That was something I was going to have to get used to because I was usually the one at home, clearing the breakfast plates and cleaning the kitchen, perusing the web for job opportunities, or heading for my afternoon shift at the bookstore. I did miss Greer's because it was the place where I first met Jamie and where I was given a job by a kind man who told me to follow my dreams even though I was certainly not the best employee. I made a mental note to visit when I lacked a bit of creative energy.

I glanced down at my wristwatch to make sure that I was early. I didn't want to be late for my first day, and I made sure to come prepared because I knew the moment I walked through the door, Victoria was going to call me into her office, asking for my drafts. I clutched the file in my purse tightly to my chest, listening to the steady stream of music coming from the radio as we pulled up in front of the skyscraper building. I was intimidated, to say the least, but I knew this was what I wanted from the moment I stepped foot into the city, and I was going to do everything in my power to make sure it counted.

I walked through the marble lobby, swiping my card and heading into the elevator up to the floor that housed Blank Page. The moment the elevator door opened, I was hit with a comforting scent of lavender from the diffuser in the entryway. The name of the magazine was etched into stone above the glass doors. I entered feeling like an entirely new woman. I was met by an intern who was standing at the door with a steaming cup of coffee in her hands. I had no idea who she had been waiting for, but when I greeted her and walked past her, she began to follow me.

"Oh, is this for me?" I asked her, and she smiled kindly.

"Yes, it is. I'm sorry. Today is my first day, as well. I've been told to help you with whatever you may need, Ms. Harlow," she said, and I could tell that she was probably a University student, excited to have her internship in a place that had so much potential.

"Please, call me Audrey. I didn't expect I would have any of that just yet, especially not on my first day. I'm just a columnist," I said, and she laughed.

"You're not just a columnist, Audrey. You're the columnist that was hand-picked by the Editor-in-Chief, Victoria herself. That means more around here than you know, but as I said earlier, I'm here to assist you with whatever you may need," she said again, and I smiled at her politely while she handed me the coffee cup, leading me over to my cubicle.

"I'm sorry, I didn't catch your name," I said.

"My name is Elle."

"It's nice to meet you, Elle."

"Before I forget, Victoria wants you in her office. She told me to tell you that you better have your first drafts of the column ready to go for the online publication," said Elle, and I nodded.

"All ready to go and on schedule. I'll head in to see her now," I said, and Elle trotted off, dealing with a bunch of mundane tasks

This was the first time that I had a real position anywhere. I never managed to stay in one place long enough to climb the ranks, but this was finally my chance to change that. I headed into Victoria's office, knocking lightly on the door while she motioned for me to come in and sit. She was on the phone, yelling at someone. I sat there quietly, waiting for her to finish.

"I hope you have your drafts ready," she said.

"I have a few for you to pick from," I said, handing her the file with each printed story proudly displayed on their separate pages.

She skimmed through them, nodding her head and lowering her glasses to the bridge of her nose, but I couldn't read her expression. I couldn't tell if she was enjoying them or if she was ready to toss them in the expensive trash can at the other end of her desk.

"These have potential, especially this one about your run-in with one of New York's most notable families. I hear that you're dating Jamie Forrest now, and that is something you can certainly write about in the future, but this piece about the family dynamic of the rich has a good angle. Tighten it up and speak from the heart because your readers are going to want to hear what you think, Audrey. Get to work. It needs to be done first thing tomorrow," she said, and I smiled.

"What are you waiting for? Go," she instructed, and I hopped up out of my seat, taking the file from her and heading back to my desk so I could start reworking the piece immediately.

I read it over for what felt like ages before my mind flooded with memories of the night that inspired this story and how terrible I had felt afterward. It was certainly a learning experience, and even though I wasn't ready to name the family I had spoken of, I was sure that some of my readers would catch on, especially once everyone realized I was dating Jamie.

I don't know how Victoria even knows about that, but I suppose news travels fast around these parts, especially in a place like this. It pays to know your stuff.

I typed away at my computer, and out of the corner of my eye, I could've sworn I saw what looked like Theodore Forrest strolling right into Victoria's office. I did a double-take, calling for Elle to come over because I had to be sure that it was him. What the hell was he doing here? I wondered why Jamie's father would be talking to a bright, thirty-some-thing magazine editor and what a man like him would even want at a place like this.

"Elle?"

"Yes, Audrey?"

"Is that Mr. Forrest? Like Jamie Forrest's father?" I asked. I couldn't quite see from how far my cubicle was away from Victoria's office.

"Yes, and I'm sure you know that because you are dating Jamie, after all," said Elle.

"Does everyone really know everything around here?" I asked, and she nodded. "I know I shouldn't even be asking you this, but you might be able to fly under the radar much more than I can right now. I need you to find out what he's doing here and why he's talking to Victoria. I feel rather uneasy about his presence."

"Leave it to me. I'll find out everything you need to know," Elle said, and I let her know how much I appreciated everything she was doing.

I had no idea how to act, having an intern be my tempo-rary assistant until Victoria was sure she was keeping me around. My stomach turned at the thought of why Jamie's father would be roaming these halls, especially since he had no business in publishing. He was supposedly a jack of all trades. Was he expanding his businesses by taking up stakes in Blank Page? I sure hoped Elle could find something substantial because I was not sure that Jamie was going to like hearing about this.

I was still worried about the conversation we had a few

days ago when he told me he spotted Eric having a suspicious chat with a stranger that made him miss a very important meeting at work. The day of the launch party was fast approaching, and I couldn't wait to get Cece alone for a few moments to grill her on what she knew about what Eric was up to. It couldn't be anything good, and I had to keep an eye out to see if the visits became a regular thing. Then, Jamie would have to have a talk with his father. None of this seemed right.

I spent the day finishing up the work I had to do. I finished my piece and had Elle drop it off on Victoria's desk. It was my first day here, but I couldn't help but feel uneasy, knowing that there was something strange going on. I could feel it in my gut. I decided to take my mind off of it because I promised Claire that I was going to be her date at one of her work functions. She was going to drink a lot and scope out the single lawyers. I had called to ask if Jamie wanted to join me, but he texted me back, saying he was going to be working late and that he wished he could've come with me. I was starting to miss him, even though it had only been a few days since we last spent any time together. I was genuinely looking forward to him accompanying me to the magazine launch party on Friday.

I knew he had a lot going on, but I was grateful that he still managed to make time for me, no matter how chaotic his life seemed to get. I packed up my things to leave the office, bidding Elle goodbye for the day while she was getting ready to go to one of her lectures. I remembered what it was like being her age. I had been wide-eyed and full of hopes that I would break onto the scene as a writer after not having tried much. After making the big move to the city, I knew following my dreams was going to be a lot harder than that. I was just grateful to be where I was. If I'd told myself a few months ago that I was going to end up working at a new magazine as a columnist, telling the kind of stories I'd been writing alone in my room for years, I would've never believed it.

I thought back to how I felt after the night when everything that Jamie and I had built together crashed and burned. I remembered how his family, Cece, and everyone else there did everything they could to tear me apart. I thought I was stronger than to take what they said to heart, but I remembered what it was like getting dressed up every day and trying to impress people who were never going to accept me, anyway. I finally had a chance to get what I wanted out of life without having to stoop to their level. I still had a lot planned, and Jamie and I'd been operating on the idea of writing an exposé book for a very long time. It might have been on the back burner for the time being, but that didn't mean I wasn't still drawing inspiration for it every chance I got.

I knew that Cece was going to come across that story eventually, picking up the new magazine with those freshly manicured fingers of hers, just to see that the new columnist was me. I wondered what would go through her head. She would probably wonder how I managed to get a position like that without her help. There was a time she had promised me the world, but she never delivered. She took back all of the opportunities she gave me just because I stood up for Jamie when his family was doing everything in their power to keep him locked up and following their rules like he was still a teenager.

It was sick to watch their attempt at control, but Jamie had much bigger problems than just trying to separate himself from his family now. His family's business was in danger, and he was doing everything he could to prevent it from becoming a sinking ship so his father could finally see that he had what it took to make it on his own. That was all he'd ever wanted, and I could only hope that he was going to get to live out his dreams one day the same way I was now living out mine.

I returned home that evening, tossing my bag onto the couch while Claire came in right after me. She smiled at me, raising her eyebrows playfully to let me know that we were going to have quite the night ahead of us, and I was looking forward to it.

"We're both going to have to get used to leaving and coming home at the same time, huh? Oh, how things change," I said, and she chuckled.

"That's right. A few months ago, you were still waiting for the right opportunity to take a chance on yourself again, and who was the one that pushed you to get yourself back out there?" she asked.

"That would be you. Go ahead, take the credit. If it weren't for you, I probably wouldn't be in this position right now. As excited as I am, I still have a lot left to worry about," I said, and she stopped in her tracks as she was venturing off to her bedroom to get changed.

"What is it? Is it Jamie?" Claire asked.

"Not exactly. I saw his father at the office today. I have no idea what he would be doing at a place like Blank Page. He's never shown a single interest in anything involving publishing, and I didn't think that he would start now. It was strange because it was the only time in the entire day that Victoria lowered the blinds in her office to give them privacy. I sent my intern to hopefully find out what was going on without bringing any attention to my prying," I said, and she stared back at me blankly.

"Wait, you have an intern?"

"Temporarily, at least until Victoria can be sure that my column is going to do well, but for now, I'm enjoying all the perks. It feels good. We can worry about all of that another time. Right now, we're getting dressed, and we're heading to your lawyer party to scope out a potential date for you," I teased.

"It's a function, and that's not what we're doing, at all. This is a professional event," she teased.

"Are you sure about that?" I asked, and she just smiled.

We both went off into our rooms to have a quick shower and get dressed. I pulled my hair back into a low ponytail, painting my lips a crisp shade of red. I slid into my figure-hugging black dress. I was just slipping into my heels when I heard my cell phone ring.

"Hello?"

"Hello, beautiful. How was your first day?" Jamie asked, and it was so good to hear his voice after the day I'd had. I debated telling him right then about seeing his father in the office, but I decided to wait to see if it happened again before I told him, just in case it was a one-time occurrence.

"It was much more exciting than I thought it would be. I really am so happy there, and now I just have to wait and see if my column is going to do well. That's the only thing that's going to solidify my position at the magazine," I said, and I knew I'd hear his praise on the other end of the line before he even said anything.

"Your column is going to do amazing, and you're going to continue having an incredible time there. That is if the other writers don't eat you alive first," he teased, and I couldn't help but laugh.

"I know you're really busy tonight, but I wish you were coming with me to this thing. I have no idea how to network with a bunch of lawyers," I said.

"Oh, it's probably a good thing that I'm not there tonight. Besides, you are Claire's wing-woman tonight if I'm not mistaken."

"That is true," I replied, smiling.

"I'll check in with you tomorrow, Audrey. Have a lovely night," he said.

"You too, Jamie."

I beamed, heading back out into the living room to find Claire waiting for me. I could tell that she was nervous to head out.

"How do I look?" she asked.

"You look incredible. Now, you need to give me a few pointers on how to make good conversation with your lawyer friends because I have absolutely no idea what I'm doing," I confessed.

"You'll figure it out. You're my wing-woman, remember?"

"How did you—"

"Next time, you should probably take your boyfriend off speaker. I noticed you didn't tell him about your little mishap at the office today, seeing his dad have a shady meeting with your boss," Claire said, and I shook my head.

"I don't think I should tell him much of anything unless I see it happen one more time. I don't want to worry him for no reason, especially because he already has so much on his plate to deal with," I said, and she nodded.

"That sounds fair. All right, let's go hail a cab."

"Right behind you."

~

ARRIVING AT THE GRAND townHOUSE, I WAS SURPRISED to see that this was the venue of choice, but Claire nudged me, letting me know that it belonged to one of the partners, and they were going to be the target of interest for the evening.

"How many partners are there at your firm?"

"Two. One of them lives here, and the other lives in that fancy apartment building downtown, the one that Jamie lives at, actually," she said, and that's when my mind started ticking away, wondering if there was even the slightest chance that it was the same man that Jamie had told me about seeing go into the elevator up to the eleventh floor. I didn't think that Claire would know what floor he lived on, but there was no harm in asking.

"Claire, do you happen to know what floor the other partner at your firm lives on?" I asked, bracing for an answer, even though I was quite sure she wasn't going to give me one. To my surprise, she told me with incredible nonchalance.

"Eleventh, I believe. Why? Oh, wait, does this have something to do with Eric?" she asked, but before I could answer, the door opened to reveal a beautiful woman, who I guessed was Elizabeth, the first partner in question.

"Ah, Claire! I'm so glad you're here, and who is this?" she asked kindly.

"This is Audrey. She's a columnist who writes for a new magazine that's launching this Friday," Claire said, smiling back at me.

"Welcome, both of you. I hope you two enjoy your evening," she said, letting us roam about the place as we pleased.

Now, time to find the other partner.

CHAPTER SEVEN: JAMIE

I received a message from one of the board members, congratulating me on my performance in the last meeting and for carrying some of the most significant financial decisions the company was going to make that year alone. It felt good to have my work recognized by someone, even if my father planned on remaining incredibly quiet about it all. I wasn't too concerned, however, because I still had Eric to worry about, and the secret meetings that happened nearly every day at the same time. I was surprised that he didn't seem scared that he was going to run into me, even though he probably knew that was going to happen at some point. I decided it was time to hit him where it hurt, invite him out, entice him with a little booze, and see if he was willing to start talking.

You may think that you're one step ahead of us all, Eric, but you're the only one that's going to fall for something like this, and I have to be grateful that you're just that gullible.

I pulled out my phone and sent a single text that told him I was in the mood for a wild night. I knew him well enough to know that he was going to jump at the first sound of that because there was nothing he liked more than partying alongside his best friend, no matter where his priorities were now. I was surprised to receive a text back quickly, asking me the time and place. I had to take him to a new spot, somewhere that would entice him enough to get wasted because it was the only way I was going to get any information out of him. I heard that there was a new club opening downtown that would be the perfect place to pull something like this off, so I ran the idea by him, and he took the bait.

My day went on as usual, and it wasn't long before Eric was knocking on the door of my office, trying to scope out whether I was serious about us hanging out later that evening.

"Weren't you the one that said this party lifestyle wasn't your thing anymore?" he asked.

"Weren't you the one that told me I needed to stop being so uptight and just let loose every once in a while?" I returned, and he ran his fingers through his hair, grinning at me while he took a seat in the chair in front of my desk.

"To be honest, heading down to a club opening is exactly what I need right now," Eric said.

"What's the matter? You've been missing work, and any time I do see you, you look so distraught. Everyone's starting to whisper about you just like they whisper about me."

"That's not true, and you know it," he said, raising his eyebrow, trying to tell if I was serious or not.

"It's true. Ask anyone that's too afraid to lose their job, and they'll tell you what the office gossip has been. You're not going to like it, and I know you're a man of your reputation. Whatever it is that's bothering you, I'm sure it can wait a single night while we go out like old times. I'll be honest, Eric, I've started to miss it. I hate hanging around here all day, being ridiculed by my father, only to realize that he's never going to change his opinion of me. It's always going to be the same level of disappointment, so sue me if I need a drink every once in a while," I said, playing the part perfectly. I watched him melt at the mention of the idea as though he couldn't wait to drink himself sick and get laid.

"Fine. Count me in, but we're going to do this my way. If I leave the preparations up to you, it's going to be far too boring. So, meet me outside that new club right at midnight, and we can even bust out our old little black book," he offered, and I nodded my head, trying to pretend to be excited about it.

"Unless your girlfriend is going to have a problem with it," he said, alluding to Audrey because he knew that we were still involved.

"She doesn't have to know, does she?" I asked, and he laughed.

"That's my boy!" he shouted, heading out of my office, letting me know that he was going to meet me later that evening.

I immediately texted Audrey to let her know what the plans were because the last thing I needed was this all to blow up in my face. She knew that I was trying to get Eric to talk, but I wasn't going to allow this to ruin my relationship, especially since I knew how capable he was of doing that. People like him and Cece knew how to get in people's heads, and they were able to do it to Audrey before.

I promised myself that I was going to protect her from all of that because she didn't deserve to get caught in the middle again, especially now that we'd grown so close. I knew she was doing everything she could to keep an eye out for any suspicious behavior, but no matter what she did, there was no way she was going to get as close as I could. I hated having to dip back into my old life for this, but it was the only way that I could be convincing enough to earn Eric's trust back. That was the only way that he was going to tell me anything, and I needed him to talk sooner rather than later. I sat there, tapping my pen on my desk, counting down the hours until I'd have to meet with him and get a little wild.

~

THE EVEnInG AIR WAS cooL on my SKIN WHEN I GOt out of my black town car, glancing over at the line of people waiting to get inside. I hung around for a few moments to see Eric approach, wearing his trusty leather jacket and smiling at me like he hadn't seen me ready to do anything like this in a very long time. I could only hope that I would be able to control myself because the last time I agreed to meet him anywhere to drink, he managed to subdue me enough to make me look bad at work. That made my father much angrier at me, worried that I was falling back into old habits again. It took him quite a while to let go of that theory, and I was starting to worry that it might happen again if I wasn't careful.

Eric and I approached the bouncer, who took one look at us and let us in without another word. I listened to the crowd of disappointed people behind us having to wait out in the cold until it was their time to enter. The place was lively. That was the thing about New York nightclubs on opening night—everyone who was anyone would make sure to show their faces. I took one look around the room and recognized a number of people I really didn't feel like talking to, so I nudged Eric, letting him know that we were probably better off in the back of the club, drinking ridiculously expensive alcohol without any prying eyes.

From the moment Eric got his first drink in him, it was like he was an entirely different person. He was letting loose, flirting with just about anyone who remotely looked in his direction. It was quite a sight to see. It was a hard pill for me to swallow, knowing that I had genuinely been like him in the past. I didn't care what I did, who I upset, or which fight I got into when I was younger. It was all about the thrill back then, but I'd grown so much since then that even I was surprised at how far I'd come.

"Another round of shots, Jamie? It feels good to have you back, man. I was wondering when you were going to get over me sleeping with your girl. I told you that we were both drunk, and we didn't mean for it to happen, but you didn't care. I get it, you were hurt, but I'm just glad that we were able to fix things now because there are great things in store for us both," he said, and I couldn't understand why he was so secretive when he wanted me to trust him.

I wanted to start pressing him right then for answers, but I knew I had to get back to playing the part—downing drinks, acting completely out of character for me, making sure that everyone in the room was aware that we were there and were having a much better time than they were. I could see a look of genuine happiness wash across Eric's face like he'd been waiting for this moment ever since he got back in the city, and it was the first time I'd seen the side of him that I missed, the side that was authentically him.

I knew there was no room for him in my life anymore, not after everything he'd done to betray me time and time again. I knew he was out to get me, but I just wasn't sure if that had anything to do with my father's company. If the Richfields were planning to pull one over on my father, they were going to have a hard time seeing it through with me around. I had to make sure that whatever Eric had been planning never saw the light of day because I was sure that the news alone was going to make us crumble.

He was starting to loosen up, and just before I started asking some of the hard-hitting questions that had been swimming around in my mind for the last hour, I saw a familiar face standing in the far back near the bar. She approached us, clutching the ends of her expensive faux fur coat, batting her eyelashes at us like she was truly surprised to see us there together, enjoying ourselves.

"Well, well. Why didn't I get an invite to this little celebration? I see that you two are friends again, and it's about time because I was getting bored of toying with only one of you," Cece said, scooting into the booth next to me. I was sandwiched between the two of them with nowhere to go.

"At least she's honest," Eric said, and I noticed he was starting to slur his words, continuing to finish glass after glass, not caring whether or not he was going to wake up right there the next morning.

"Cece, I thought we might run into you here tonight," I said, trying not to pay her too much attention because it was the one thing she couldn't live without.

"You were hoping to run into me then? I suppose there had to be someone to drag you both home when this was all over. I know how wild nights out with the two of you can get, or have you forgotten about all the fun we used to have, Jamie?" she asked, trying to remind me of a time when I certainly wasn't myself.

I had no choice but to play along. I could tell that Cece was testing me, and she probably had a little deal with Eric to get me distracted, but I wasn't wasted in the slightest. I was paying very close attention to every little detail.

"How could I forget, Cece? There was a time when I used to be able to tolerate you. Sadly, I'm having a bit of trouble with that these days. Though tonight has been all about forgiveness, and if I can forgive Eric, then I suppose there's some room for forgiveness for you, too," I said, lying through my teeth, but she was a smart one, asking all the right questions.

"Oh yeah, and how does your little writer girlfriend feel about that?"

"In Jamie's words, he said she doesn't have to know," Eric chimed in.

"Well then, I guess we better keep this our little secret."

CHAPTER EIGHT: AUDREY

I stared down at my cell phone and reread the text message that Jamie sent me. I hoped he was going to be okay. I'd heard stories about how he acted whenever he was in those situations, and having rescued him from the club that night only made me worry more. I tried to focus because I had to find the second partner at Claire's firm, get a good look at the guy, and see if he was the same person who was talking to Eric. If Eric was consulting with the partner at a law firm, then whatever he was up to couldn't be any good.

I filled Claire in on all the missing details while we both looked around the room. She had to be the one to introduce me to him because he knew her well. I didn't want him to remember me much, especially if I was going to do a bit of digging.

"What's his name again?" I asked, whispering in Claire's ear.

"His name is Michael Pierson, and he's a dick," she whispered back as we moved through the party.

I stayed right behind her, waiting for her to recognize him, and it wasn't long before she was pointing at a man standing near the fireplace with a glass of whiskey in his hand. His beard was perfectly trimmed, his suit was ridiculously expensive, and he had the kind of smile that would tell anyone that he was up to something. I sighed, pulling out my cell phone at a safe distance away and taking a picture of him. I sent the photo to Jamie, wanting to know if he had been the one that he saw in the lobby of his building. I waited patiently, sipping my drink and pretending to mingle alongside my best friend while I scrolled through my phone, anticipating Jamie's text. I looked down at the screen when it came in, confirming my suspicions. That was him. I had no idea how I was going to play this, but as far as Michael knew, I was just another woman at the party, looking for a handsome lawyer to talk to.

"Quick, Claire. What does Michael like to talk about? I'm going to try to flirt a little and fish around for some information. Let's just hope that he has absolutely no idea who I am," I said, and she nodded.

"He wouldn't know who you are unless he saw you himself, and I don't think you two have had a run-in just yet, so let's change that. The man likes to talk about his job, about his life, and anything concerning himself, so just pretend to be interested in that," she said, coaching me well before she led me to him.

The moment he laid eyes on me, he smiled. It wasn't a smile of recognition. I thought he probably thought I was just another girl he was going to take back to his apartment to sleep with, but he was wrong. I could already tell a man like him liked a challenge. He wouldn't stop until he got me to pay close attention to every move he made, playing me for a fool the same way he probably did to a lot of people in the courtroom. I held my head high while Claire introduced us, and I smiled coyly back at him, waiting for him to show some interest.

"Well, Claire. You didn't tell me that this best friend of yours was so beautiful. Can I get you something to drink, Audrey?" he asked, and I nodded.

"That would be lovely, thank you," I said, and Michael led me off to where the bar was, asking for my preference.

"Surprise me," I said, and he winked at me, finishing his drink so he could join me with a fresh one.

The look on his face was incredibly predatory. He was just waiting for the right moment to swoop in and promise me if I spent a night with him, he would give me everything I could ever dream of. Claire warned me about men like him, the ones that felt far too powerful for their own good, but I was playing along for the time being because I needed to know what he was really up to and how his connection to Eric impacted Jamie.

"So, tell me, Audrey, what do you do?"

"I'm a columnist at this up and coming magazine that's launching this Friday, actually. It's an exciting move but probably not as exciting as commanding a courtroom," I said, sipping on the drink in my hand that was far too strong.

"It's not all bells and whistles, trust me. Half of the time, I'm wishing I didn't have to deal with some of the cases that come in, especially when it comes to helping out a friend. I'll tell you this, and you can feel free to warn Claire, but it's best us lawyers stay away from the big sharks in the business world. They're always trying to get us to find loopholes where there aren't any," he confessed, and I knew he was talking about Eric. I just couldn't figure out why yet.

"Big sharks, huh? They sound terrifying, probably the kind that would demand you make a loophole when you can't find one," I said, watching his brows furrow. He shot me a look that told me he was impressed by my perceptions.

"Now, I didn't think I would ever run into a woman that

felt the same way I do about these things. Maybe I should be the one asking you for advice," he said, and I forced a laugh, waiting for him to tell me exactly what he knew.

"I'm sure I could offer some sort of advice to help you out. Claire has been a good teacher, and let's just say I've always been interested in how you lawyer men manage to get away with such things. There isn't a way that it's all perfectly legal, right?" I asked teasingly as I bit my lip. I could see the hunger in his eyes, and he was truly prepared to tell me anything I needed to know. I had him right where I wanted him, and it was finally time that someone started getting some answers around here.

"I have this friend. He's a total dick, but I promised him I'd help him get his foot through the door. Apparently, his parents signed a deal that gave him the perfect opportunity. He just needed a way to get everyone out of the way so he could make his mark," he said, and I was sure he was talking about Eric.

"Yes, he certainly sounds like a dick. Well, I'm sure you're going to help him get everything he needs to succeed. I'll be sure to call you if I ever need representation, but unfortunately, I don't have your number," I said, and he chuckled, pulling out his phone for me to put it in.

"Michael!" I heard Elizabeth scream from the other end of the room.

"Go ahead, put it in, and you can leave it on the mantle when you're done. I'll be back in a moment," he said, blindly trusting me because he truly believed that I couldn't be any harm to him and his precious little secrets.

I waited until the coast was clear, and Claire came up to me right as I was going through his call log and text messages, getting all the evidence I needed to stop Eric in his tracks. It was clear as day what his plans were. He was going to try to crumble Forrest Industries, and he was going to pave the way for the Richfields to take their place. I realized it was much worse than I thought, and once I managed to get a copy of everything I needed, I placed the phone down on the mantle, making sure to leave my number in there just in case we'd need to lure him out.

I tried to enjoy the rest of the evening, but I wanted to storm out of there, go to wherever Jamie was, and fill him in on all the terrible details I learned. I knew I had to let him try to get a few answers out of Eric before we confronted them both. We couldn't allow the Richfields to take charge of Forrest Industries, no matter how much control Theodore Forrest gave them so that they could grow together. For a man that couldn't even trust his own son, he sure did a great job of trusting the wrong people. I wondered what lies the Richfields told him to get him to sign the deal in the first place. I worried that we were going to be too late to fix any of this because if Eric already had such a powerful lawyer on his side, it was only a matter of time before everything came crashing down.

I was just glad that Michale had been the typical, predictable kind of man that had absolutely no idea who I was. The moment he found that out, he was going to feel stupid for allowing himself to be played like that. I hoped that we were going to be able to get this information to Jamie's father before the Richfields made any moves that would make it impossible for him to regain control of his own company. Those contracts were solid, just as solid as the one he made Jamie sign when he was still young and still impressionable enough to listen to whatever his father had to say.

I sent Jamie a text message that told him that we needed to talk and that it was urgent, but I didn't get a response this time. I had a terrible feeling in the pit of my stomach. I worried Eric had managed to regain control like last time he and Jamie had gone out, but I could only hope that Jamie was going to come out on top this time. If Jamie managed to get Eric wrapped around his finger again, there was a good chance we would be able to stop this from happening, even if we weren't too sure what this was yet. It had to be big if Eric got Michael involved, but I wasn't going to let him bend the rules for anyone, especially when it came to protecting Jamie's family, no matter how dysfunctional they were. Jamie had to be the one that pulled Forrest Industries out of this so his father would finally tear up that contract and let him go.

We're going to get through this, Jamie. We're going to do this together.

~

I HEADED HOME THAt EVEnInG FEELING BOTH confused and like everything I'd come to learn was now starting to make sense. Claire and I sat on the couch for what felt like hours, going through every detail we could think of and trying to make sense of it all. It seemed like we'd stumbled upon the answer that was going to make everything okay and was going to lead us straight to what Eric had planned for Forrest Industries. I still had no idea how he planned on forcing everyone out because he surely couldn't do it alone.

The only way that he could pull off something like that was if he proved to the board that both Theodore and Jamie were unfit to lead the company forward. I wondered if Eric would really stoop to that level to get what he wanted, but I knew better than to question it. He certainly seemed like the type to do just about anything to take what he could from his best friend. Their problems started when he managed to entice Cece enough to sleep with him, trying to convince Jamie that it had been a mistake all along.

Jamie had told me that he wasn't too surprised that Cece did something like that, but what surprised him was that his best friend would be capable of something like that after having known each other since they were children. I couldn't imagine Claire doing that to me, and I knew that was exactly how Jamie must've felt. I had a familiar feeling of unease, especially because I hadn't heard from Jamie for the rest of the evening. I curled up on the couch, throwing a blanket over my legs, hanging around by my cell phone as I waited for a response that came. I grew even more worried that Eric managed to get Jamie right where he wanted him because even though Jamie promised me that he would be careful, that didn't mean that Eric didn't come prepared.

I slept it off, trying to calm myself down because if I started blowing up his phone, it was certainly going to give Eric the wrong idea. I didn't want to mess things up for Jamie, especially if he'd spent the entire night trying to get Eric to trust him again. I told myself that I would stop by his suite before work in the hopes that he would be curled up in bed, ready to tell me everything he'd learned.

When I finally woke and got ready for the day, I couldn't help but feel my stomach turn like something wasn't right. I bid Claire goodbye as we both took off in opposite directions in separate cabs, trying to make the best of the day. She'd told me not to worry, but I truly couldn't help myself. I was so scared that something happened to Jamie, and even more so now that I was pulling up to his building, unsure of what I was going to find when I finally made it inside. Everything seemed normal when I swiped the keycard that Jamie had made for me and entered into his suite, but then I was hit with a waft of familiar perfume that certainly wasn't my own.

"I wondered when you would try to show your face again," Cece said, wearing one of Jamie's button-down shirts and her hair a mess like she just had another wild night.

I glanced over into the bedroom to see Jamie fast asleep. My heart sank into my stomach at the thought that he would've gone to such lengths, sleeping with her to get the answers he wanted. At that moment, I thought maybe I didn't know Jamie at all. Maybe everything we'd been trying to do together was all for nothing. It hurt my heart, knowing that he could do something like that and not even bother to think about me. There was no other explanation this time, and there was no way that Cece could've pulled a fast one over on me, even if I wanted to believe that was the case. There he was, sound asleep, his breathing calm as though he was enjoying the rest he was getting after the incredible night they had together.

"What are you doing here?" I asked angrily.

"Jamie and I got a little hot and heavy last night. I knew he was going to get bored of you and come running back to someone a little more his speed. I didn't think he would've done it before speaking to you first because he's always been the good one, but I guess that you've changed him, Audrey. He obviously doesn't care about you anymore. So, why don't you take the hint and get out of his life for good? He doesn't want you here, and I certainly don't want you here, so you should probably leave that key on your way out," she said, and I felt the tears begin to well up behind my eyes.

I slammed the key down on the table, feeling the rage course through my veins as I slammed the suite door and ran through the corridor back to the elevator so I could get out of there. This was the last thing that I thought Jamie would do. He promised me he was going to protect me from all of this and that he was going to stand by me no matter what, and he threw all that away just so he could further his own agenda. Maybe he was not the man I thought he was, after all. Maybe I should've left when I had the chance. Tears began to flow freely from my eyes, streaming down my face as I wiped them away and hailed a cab.

I didn't think I'd ever been that angry in my entire life, and I didn't know how to process any of it. It was far too much for me to handle, and now I wasn't sure if I wanted to share the information I'd learned at the firm's party I attended with Claire. I wasn't going to willfully clean up Jamie's messes for him if he couldn't stay faithful to me. I couldn't believe he allowed Cece to weasel her way back into his life, and now I knew that he was just as bad as everyone else. Now, it was time I looked out for myself.

CHAPTER NINE: JAMIE

My head hurt so much worse than I thought possible, and I started to think that maybe I'd let things get a little too out of hand last night. It was a complete bust, and Eric didn't offer me any information that could point me in the right direction of what was really going on. I had to keep pushing and keep trying to find out the truth because I genuinely felt something terrible had been in the works for quite some time. I had to get to the bottom of what that is.

I rubbed my eyes as I tossed and turned between my sheets, thankful that I at least made it back home in one piece. I reached over to my nightstand for my phone, looking at the last text message that Audrey sent, which let me know that she found something and we needed to talk. I knew she and I had a lot of catching up to do, especially after she managed to find out who the mysterious man was that Eric had been meeting with. It was probably time I had a chat with him myself because if he was the one helping Eric orchestrate this whole mess, it was time that someone finally put him in his place.

I got up from my bed, rubbing the back of my neck while I walked over to the kitchen to start a pot of coffee, but my eyes widened when I saw that it was already made. I could smell the scent of a familiar perfume around the place, and I watched the hallway bathroom door swing open to reveal Cece. Her hair was wet, dripping on my carpet, wrapped up in one of my towels. I was more shocked than I had been in a very long time because I knew for a fact that she and I parted ways last night after I realized that I wasn't going to get anywhere with either of them.

"What are you doing in my suite? Do I need to call security, Cece?" I asked, inching towards the phone, but she shook her head.

"You don't remember what happened last night, do you, Jamie?" she asked, biting her lips, trying to get me to remember something that didn't happen.

"I don't remember what happened, Cece, because nothing did. However you managed to get in here, I'm sure you can find your clothes and get out," I said, not even bothering to deal with her.

"That's funny because your girlfriend stopped by earlier this morning, and she told me that she didn't mind if I stayed," said Cece, and just like that, my blood started to boil yet again.

"What do you mean, Audrey was here? What the hell did you do, Cece?"

"I just reminded her that she was never going to fit in around here and that she is not the kind of girl that you're ever going to have a future with. We had a lot of fun last night, and it reminded me of all the good times when we'd wake up right here in this suite together, excited to go on living our rich, fruitful lives," she said, and I couldn't believe how bold she was.

"You've made quite a mess while trying to enact your

sick, twisted fantasy, Cece. There is no place for you or anyone like you in my life ever again. I haven't needed someone like you since I realized that I wanted more out of life than a shallow, washed up socialite who was never going to find any sort of success in life. Your only characteristic is spending the money that your parents gave you, and that is so sad. Maybe it's time you stop meddling in other people's business and take a good long look at yourself," I said, and I could see the hurt in her eyes, but she tried her best to brush it off.

"You don't mean that, Jamie. I know there's a part of you that still loves me and still cares about me, and I'm not going to stop until I remind you just how much you miss me," she said, dropping her towel so I could get an eyeful of her toned, naked body.

I glanced over to the couch, gathered the folded set of clothes I assumed belonged to her, and I tossed them in her direction. She scoffed, trying to understand how I could be so cruel to her. It was because the only person that she could ever think about was herself.

"Get out of my suite before I have to get someone up here to escort you out," I warned, and she listened.

I watched her get dressed while she wore that sulking facial expression of hers, trying to get me to feel bad for her, but I had no time for her manipulation. I was far too concerned with the fact that Audrey was out there some-where, probably thinking that I had done the very same thing to her that Cece had done to me all those years ago. I could only hope that I found her in time to fix things. Otherwise, I knew I was going to have quite a lot of regrets.

She left without another word, and I got dressed as fast as I could while dialing Audrey's number. She didn't answer. I ran down to the concierge, told her what happened, and asked for them to make sure that no one ever had access to my suite again. I couldn't allow this to happen, knowing that there was always going to be a chance that something came between Audrey and me, whether it was Eric, my father, or Cece. My blood was boiling as I called the car around to take me straight to Audrey's office. I had to let her know that I didn't do anything. I put myself in her shoes for a moment, wondering how I would've reacted to seeing something like that, knowing I would've acted out before I even managed to get an explanation.

I let my guard down for one minute, thinking that everything was going to be fine, and Cece found her way inside of my suite to trick my girlfriend into thinking I slept with her. That was all all-time low, even for Cece. I had my chauffeur take the fastest route there. When I finally got to the front desk, I was met by a young intern who stared at me blankly, trying to figure out what I was doing here.

"Jamie Forrest?" she asked, and I smiled, trying to be polite before I allowed myself to take my anger out on this poor girl.

"That would be me. I'm looking for Audrey. I really need to talk to her. It's important," I said, and she shook her head at me, staring back at me like she was about to deliver some bad news.

I didn't care. I wasn't going to leave until I had a moment alone with her, until I could convince her that nothing happened. This was exactly what Cece wanted. At that moment, I didn't even care where Eric was or what he'd been up to. I had to fix things with the girl I was falling in love with before it was too late.

"She gave me strict instructions to turn you away if you showed up here. Shame on you, sir," said the girl, but I wasn't going to allow her to keep me from seeing Audrey.

"Everything that Audrey may have told you was a big misunderstanding, and I really need to see her so I can explain myself. Please, I'm begging you," I said, and it was the first time I'd fought so hard to get past anyone, but she eventually let me pass.

"Her cubicle is right down that way. Make it quick. I don't want Victoria to catch you here," she said.

"Thank you, uh—"

"Elle.

"Thank you, Elle," I said, rushing to find Audrey.

When I got to her cubicle, she was nowhere to be found. I glanced directly across to see that she was sitting in Victoria's office. I'd never met the woman in person, but I heard enough to know who she was. I wanted to heed Elle's warning about not letting her see me, but I just couldn't help myself, so I rushed over to the glass office door and knocked lightly until I was told to come in.

"I'm truly sorry to interrupt, and you don't know me, but I really need to talk to Audrey," I said, and Audrey turned around, staring back at me like she was going to kill me for barging in like this.

"I know exactly who you are, Jamie Forrest, as do half the people in this city. I've just finished up with Audrey. You two may go," she said kindly, and I thanked her even though there was a part of me that worried I may have ruffled her feathers a little too much.

Audrey dragged me out of the office into the corridor, her face an expression of anger that I'd never seen before. I knew she had every right to be angry because she didn't know the truth.

"What are you doing here, Jamie? I really don't want to see you right now. Besides, don't you have another girlfriend to get back to?" she spat, and I gazed into her eyes, caressing her cheek so she could get a good look at my expression while I told her that everything Cece did to set us up was completely out of malicious intent.

"Audrey, I need you to believe me when I tell you that nothing happened between Cece and me. I know that's hard to believe, but I woke up today to find her in my room, and I had no idea how she even managed to get in there. I made sure to tell security to blacklist her from the building, but I had no idea that she was there or that you two spoke. I promise you that nothing happened, that I never laid a hand on her. She was there at the bar with Eric and me last night, but we all parted ways when I realized I wasn't getting any more information out of her. Please, you have to believe me. I can't lose you over one of Cece's ridiculous games," I said, pleading with her as she gazed into my eyes, searching for the truth in my expression.

"I had a feeling that something was wrong, but I was just so hurt seeing her like that, in your shirt and looking like she'd just rolled out of bed from sleeping with you, that I couldn't help but react. I'm so sorry, Jamie. I know I shouldn't have jumped to conclusions like that, but—"

"You have nothing to apologize for, Audrey. I need you to understand this right now. I would never hurt you that way, or any way, for that matter. Ever since you've come into my life, I wanted to keep you by my side every step of the way. I wanted to be there for you, no matter how hard things might get, and none of that has changed. I love you, Audrey," I said, and it was the first time those words had ever left my lips to anyone. I couldn't have found a better time to tell her exactly how I felt and to let her know I wanted her to help me see this through so that we could finally get back to living our lives together.

"I love you, too, Jamie," she said, staring back at me wide-eyed.

We both realized it was finally time that we started paying a little more attention to what was happening between us. We'd had such a spark from the very beginning, and I knew it was only a matter of time before we'd find ourselves in this very position, telling each other that we couldn't imagine our lives without one another. It was the genuine truth. I pressed my lips into hers, feeling the warmth of her skin on mine while I held her there in front of everyone, letting the office know exactly how I felt about their new columnist, Audrey Harlow.

"Jamie, we need to talk. There's a lot I learned last night that gives me a reason to believe the lawyer Michael who Eric met with recently is trying to help him overthrow your father's company. Right now, we need to get this information to him as fast as possible. Otherwise, it might be too late for anyone to stop it," she said, and just like that, we were jolted back to reality.

I watched her grab her purse, telling Elle to let Victoria know that there was an emergency she needed to tend to, and we were off, heading for my father's office. I could only hope that we were going to make it in time. There was the chance something was already happening right under our noses that we had absolutely no idea about. My heart began to pound loudly in my chest as the worry began to set in that I was potentially about to lose everything I'd been working so hard to protect. The only way I was ever going to have a future of my own was if I could save my father's company from crumbling. I had to thank Audrey for finding this information, to begin with, and I promised myself to fight for my father to see her for who she truly was because she was the sole reason we even had a lead to follow.

I couldn't believe how incredible she had been and how she always managed to stand by me, no matter how difficult things seemed to get between us. There was no shortage of fascinating moments between us, and the more complicated my life got, the more I felt like she was going to wake up one day and decide that she didn't want to live this kind of life anymore. Yet, it was times like now that I realized she truly loved me, too. She wasn't going to go anywhere because she felt the same about me as I did her, and as much as I wanted to protect her from the chaos that was my life, she found her way in so she could help me take down the monsters in my life without compromising who I was and who I wanted to become.

Audrey was the one that pulled me out of my own darkness. She showed me there was a way out of all of this, even if the chances we had in the past seemed to blow up in our faces. She always convinced me to try again and never give up, regardless of how difficult things might've gotten since we'd met. I had her to thank for it all.

You've made me a better man, Audrey Harlow, and I promise that once this is all over, I will show you how much you truly mean to me, without all of this chaos surrounding us.

We got into the back of my black town car, taking off into the heart of the city, making our way back to my father's office. She rested her hand in mine, and I squeezed it tightly because I was genuinely so afraid of what we were about to walk into that I didn't know how to behave.

I was so worried that we were going to be too late and that my father was going to be forced into handing over the company to the Richfields before we had the chance to show him that this had been their plan all along. Eric wasn't back in town to make me pay for banishing him. He was back with his family behind him so they could take everything away from us. They truly believed we owed them this and that we were never supposed to be the ones to receive this much success.

I never thought Eric would have been this envious. He went to extreme lengths to make sure nothing would stand in the way of seeing this deal through, but I was about to crash this little parade of his so that I could make sure that my father wasn't forced into doing anything he would regret for the rest of his life. My father had trust issues. He would have trouble believing the family he'd known for the better half of his life would try to pull this over on him. It was time I saved him from making a terrible mistake for a change.

Hang in there, Father. We're going to stop this before it has the chance to get ugly. You have no idea what they've been planning behind your back, but you're going to learn soon enough.

CHAPTER TEN: AUDREY

I was so quick to judge Jamie when he was faithful to me all this time. I couldn't believe I allowed myself to get wrapped up in one of Cece's schemes, but she managed to play everything out perfectly, making me believe that Jamie would be capable of hurting me. The tension was high now because I didn't know if we would make it in time to stop the impending disaster, but I had to hold out hope. I was so scared that we were going to be too late and that we wouldn't make it in time to convince Mr. Forrest that he was making a terrible mistake. Worse, I was scared that he wasn't going to believe us.

Keep your head held high, Audrey. Once you see this through, you and Jamie will finally have the happiness you've been trying to explore for quite some time. You're almost there.

We pulled in front of the building moments later, and I could feel how worried Jamie was. He glanced back at me with a look of utter apprehension as we both scrambled to get up to the top floor as fast as possible. When we finally arrived on the main floor, we were stopped by the receptionist at the front as though she was told to keep us out until business was finished.

"What are you doing?" Jamie asked.

"I was told not to let you anywhere near Mr. Forrest today because the meeting he's currently in is far too important," she said with an air of such authority it even made me angry.

"I'm sorry, darling, but that's not going to happen," I chimed in, and we both pushed past her, trying to get to Mr. Forrest's office door without any other obstacles.

When we finally got there, we both stormed inside, and I glanced around the room to see the Richfields, Michael, and Theodore Forrest all gathering around the table, halting their discussion the moment they laid eyes on us.

"Father, what the hell do you think you're doing by entertaining these people?" Jamie asked.

I looked over at Michael, who had been surprised to see me. He couldn't help but realize what he had done.

"Son, I was wondering when you were going to try to ambush this meeting. Why don't you have a seat? Eric here has had a wonderful business proposal that we should all hear yet again," Mr. Forrest said, but Jamie wasn't having any of it.

"You can't possibly be entertaining this. You have no idea what they've been planning behind your back, Father. This little business venture of Eric's is his way of infiltrating the company so he can help his family steal it out from under you," Jamie said, not even bothering to hold back.

"What are you talking about?"

"I met Michael at a party that was being held in honor of their firm, and he, being a typical man in his career, tried to use his words to entice me to sleep with him. In that, he managed to tell me that he was helping a prospective client of his create a loophole where there wasn't one. I know you don't like me very much, Mr. Forrest, but know that I care about Jamie. I wouldn't want anything to happen to your business. Jamie has been through enough as it is, and his sole mission lately has been to make sure that no harm comes to you or Forrest Industries. So, before you make any decisions you're going to regret, I suggest you hear us out," I said, and he looked shocked to hear me speak to him that way, but it was the only way I was going to get him to listen.

"You were really trying to dupe me, weren't you, Eric? You know, when your father came to me with the idea of joining forces, I have to be honest, I was a little apprehensive at first, but of course, I always find a way to protect my empire. You see, you and your father didn't bother to read the contract you signed when we made our first agreement. It stated that if there are any instances where you try to harm the company or my family, the partnership will be dissolved. Did you forget about that, Pierson?" he asked, staring back at Michael, who couldn't seem to look him directly in the eye.

"Mr. Forrest, are you really going to believe your son right now? Haven't you seen the kind of behavior that he's displayed over the last few days? He's a total mess and completely unfit to be a part of this business," Eric said, trying his very best to get Mr. Forrest on board with his business decision.

"I have to thank my son and his girlfriend for getting here when they did because if I were to have signed my name on the dotted line, it would override the contract that we originally signed. But you knew that, didn't you?" Mr. Forrest asked, and it was the first time I ever saw him acknowledge Jamie for doing a good job.

"Please, Theo, we can work this out. I had no part in any of this underhanded business, and I'm sure we can look past anything unintentionally untoward because we've known each other for so long," Eric's father said.

"Father, you can't possibly deny you had no part in this.

This was your decision from the time you got back into the city. You wanted Forrest Industries for yourself, and I was prepared to do just about anything to get it for you," Eric confessed.

The plan he'd been brewing had blown up in his face. It was the first time I saw Eric genuinely angry like he was ready to start a fight and enact his revenge before anyone could haul him out of Mr. Forrest's office.

"I think it's time for you all to get the hell out of my office," Mr. Forrest said, and I couldn't agree more.

He reached over to his intercom, calling for security to have them escorted out and blacklisted from ever returning. It wasn't long before it was just Jamie and me standing before his father, and it was the first time I'd ever seen that man's expression soften. He motioned for us both to sit. I was worried he was going to find something new to criticize or ridicule us for, but that never happened. There was genuine appreciation in his eyes, and for the first time in a while, I didn't feel so intimidated by his presence.

"I have to thank you both for keeping me from making one of the biggest mistakes in this company's history. If you two hadn't gotten here when you did, they would've been able to regain control and take everything away from us. You see, Jamie, when I held that intervention to get you to stay, it wasn't just because I didn't want you to expose our family secrets. It was because I knew that you would find success no matter which part of the world you ended up in. I kept you back because I was selfish. I wouldn't allow anyone else to have you. I know you've been waiting for an opportunity to branch out on your own, and after today, I think that maybe there is room for compromise on both ends. I'm sure we can work something out," Mr. Forrest said, and Jamie smiled, feeling rather accomplished as he outstretched his hand to rest it in mine.

"As for you, Audrey Harlow. You don't give up, do you? My family has said some awful things to you, and we've shown you just how terrible we can act when it comes to the ones we love. Yet, you stuck by Jamie's side and helped him carry this out. You played a large role in saving this company, and I am indebted to you for that. I know you have the position at Blank Page, and I look forward to seeing just how much success you're able to come into once that magazine launches in two days. I'm sorry for the way I've acted towards you, and I know I've been blinded more times than I can count over the years, but I see now that you genuinely do care about Jamie. Thank you, Audrey," he said.

"You're welcome, sir," I said.

"Please, call me Theo."

It was a win, the first real victory Jamie and I felt since we first got together. I remembered how difficult it was for us in the beginning and how worried we had been as to if it was a good idea for us to see each other. I was so proud of Jamie for the man he'd become and how much he'd fought for what he wanted, no matter who was standing in his way. He proved to his father that he deserved more responsibility and that he was capable of making decisions that would benefit the company. It was the beginning of our happily ever after. Though there was a part of me that still worried Eric was going to come back one day to try to enact his revenge when we least expected it, but that was a problem for another day.

Jamie and I finally had what we'd always wanted, and it was time we were able to explore how we felt about each other without the worry that the chaos could get in the way. I wanted him to know I was never going to leave his side, and I was going to be there for him no matter what because he'd changed my life. He was there to help me see out my dreams, pull me back in when I was going off the deep end, and make me a better person. I never thought I would be able to coexist with someone like him in this world of his, but he'd shown me it wasn't all bad. There was still hope that we could find a middle ground. We were going to have everything we could dream of in time. Jamie was the happiest I'd ever seen him, ready to navigate this new chapter of his life with me by his side.

I couldn't wait to go to the launch party with him on my arm, knowing that we'd just fought against the bad guys and won. It was something that we'd been trying to do for so long that it felt surreal, but I was so glad we finally had a moment to ourselves to enjoy it. Jamie and I left the office feeling incredible, and I sat with him in the back of his black town car while it took me back to his suite. I could feel the tension in the air between us, and I knew it was finally time we spent the night together. After all, we had nothing else standing in our way. He glanced over at me, staring deep into my eyes as he pulled me closer.

"You saved me, Audrey Harlow, in ways you'll never be able to imagine. I love you," he said, and I smiled, pressing my lips into his and feeling his soft lips on mine, but I couldn't help but keep grinning.

"I love you so much, Jamie Forrest. This truly is a new beginning for us."

"Another wild ride that I can't wait for," he said, and I chuckled while he pulled me into his lap.

I felt his hands travel my body, letting me know what would happen once we got up the stairs to his suite. The tension was high as he led me through the door, slamming my back against the wall and kissing me. I felt his fingertips travel over every inch of my body while he helped me out of my clothes. I unbuttoned his shirt and tossed it down. I glanced down to see the pile on the floor while he picked me up, carrying me over to his bed. I felt his warm kisses trail down my neck to my décolletage, stopping at the curves of my breast while he undid my bra. His touch made me feel incredible. It ignited something in me that I had never felt before. I wanted him. I wanted all of him. This was the moment we'd been waiting for, one that we never got until now because of how chaotic his life had been.

I felt him spread my legs open, slipping my panties down as I bit my lips in anticipation, waiting for him to slide inside of me and make my entire body quiver. I felt the warmth of his skin on mine while he hovered over me, and I outstretched my hand to caress his cheek, running my fingers along his lip while he leaned in to kiss me.

"I love you, Audrey," he whispered in my ear, sliding deep inside of me.

"I love you too, Jamie," I said.

I felt every inch of him thrust in and out of me, leading me closer and closer to the orgasm that was waiting to erupt through me. Jamie made me feel like no man had ever made me feel before, and I didn't want the night to end. He'd given me everything I could ever ask for, and we were finally one step closer to exploring a future together. He changed my life in more ways than I could possibly count, and I couldn't help but bask in the pleasure of it all. We laid there together, curled up underneath his sheets, falling asleep in each other's arms as I dreamt of all the wonderful things we were going to be able to do now that we weren't under constant distress.

I heard his cell phone ring in the middle of the night, and I noticed that the caller had been Cece, so I got up from the bed where Jamie had been fast asleep and answered.

"Hello, Cece. Quite late to be calling, don't you think? Or are you still hoping that Jamie's going to take you back? I know about the little stunt you pulled here at Jamie's place. I have to be honest, you had me fooled for a moment, but let's just say we managed to work everything out," I said, waiting for her snarky response, but she sounded like she was in tears.

"What did you and Jamie do? What did you do?" she asked angrily, nearly screaming through the phone.

"What are you talking about, Cece?"

"Eric, he's gone. He and his family took off, and I can't imagine why. We were about to have a life together. We were about to have everything we could've ever wanted, and you two had to go and ruin that for us," she said, and I couldn't believe that she was this upset about Eric when just a few hours ago, she was trying to get me to think that she was sleeping with Jamie.

"We foiled his plan, which I'm sure Eric must've filled you in on. Forrest Industries is safe for another day, and I'm sorry that things didn't work out between you two. I'm sure you will find someone just as vapid and shallow as you to spend the rest of your days with," I said, taking every opportunity to get a jab in where I could.

"You better watch your mouth, Audrey. You may be Jamie's current favorite, but you still have yet to see just how often that changes. He may have you fooled into believing he's this nice guy who is going to give you everything you could ever want, but you have to remember something. We all thought we were going to be his forever girl at one time in our lives, and he broke each and every one of our hearts. It's only a matter of time before you realize that for yourself. I tried to warn you. I tried to tell you to stay away, but you just don't listen, do you? I'm going to get you back for taking Eric away from me, and you're going to wish you never got involved with Jamie or any of this," she said.

"I'd like to see you try," I replied, hanging up the phone, returning it to its place on Jamie's nightstand while I curled up in bed with him again.

I could hear the distress and frustration in Cece's voice.

She was plotting revenge of her own, and I knew that our story was far from over.

Whatever you think you know about Jamie is false, Cece. He's a different man when he's with me, and he's never given me a reason to doubt him. The only terrible people in his life seem to be you, Eric, and the Richfields. For now, we don't have to worry about any of you, and I can only hope that it stays that way.

EPILOGUE: JAMIE

In a short amount of time, my life changed so much. I'd fallen in love with a woman that made me excited to get up every day, challenged me, and stood by me when I needed her the most. Audrey was everything I could've ever asked for, and I tried every single day to remind her of how special she was to me. I was surprised that things started to change for me at work, as well. My father gave me an entire department to run on my own. He was stepping down and learning to delegate in a way I'd never seen him do before. I supposed nearly losing his entire company made him realize that he couldn't always look out for himself, especially when it came to the people he thought he trusted. I was glad Audrey and I got there at the right time to stop him from making such a terrible mistake. I could only hope that I continued to show him that I was an asset around here because now that we'd found a middle ground, I wasn't hoping I could find a new way to make him let me go.

We were starting to mend our relationship, but when it came to introducing Audrey into the rest of my world, it seemed my father was the only one that appreciated her company. I supposed it was a start, and it was all I could've asked for a few months ago. I could only hope that, with time, the rest of my family started to see that she was an amazing woman. She'd been there for me and taught me to stay strong, even when I thought I was on the verge of losing everything I'd worked so hard to protect. I knew we both still had so much to get used to. Our lives were constantly changing, but I couldn't wait to see what adventure we embarked on next. When I was next to Audrey, I felt like I could conquer the world, and I couldn't wait to stand by her at the launch of Blank Page tonight.

She'd just gotten out of the shower, looking as beautiful as ever wrapped up in a towel with her wet hair slicked back, and I couldn't help but pin her against the wall and kiss her relentlessly.

"Do we have to be this early?" I asked, wishing I could take her back to bed for another few minutes.

"I wish we didn't, but this is a big night for me, and you still haven't gotten to see me in the dress we picked out together for this occasion. Go on, get dressed. Otherwise, we're going to be late," she said with a smile, planting a soft kiss on my lips.

"We're going to be late for being early?" I asked, and she chuckled.

I caressed her cheek, pulling her in close so I could feel her kiss me before I let her venture back off into the bathroom to slip into that lovely dress of hers. It wasn't long before she came out, ready to slip into her heels for the evening.

"You look incredible, Audrey," I said, and she smiled.

"You don't look half bad, yourself," she replied.

I remembered the first time she'd used that line on me. It felt wonderful to have her on my arm. I carried her down to my black town car so that we could make it to the launch party. She'd changed so much since the first time I'd seen her, but the growth was undeniable. She'd truly come into her own, making anyone who could ever doubt her eat their words.

When we arrived, the place looked amazing. The atmosphere wasn't anything like the mundane parties my mother would throw. It was lively, the music was lovely, and the food was exquisite. I let Audrey go, watching her mingle as I stood back, watching her command the room. I couldn't wait to see just how great her column was going to be. After she'd made a slight change to the first story to include some incredible details from both of our lives, I knew it was going to be one for the ages. It was going to ruffle a lot of feathers around the community, but I didn't care anymore. I promised to stand by Audrey, and I believed in her work, even if it meant exposing a few of my family secrets every once in a while. I wasn't ashamed of who I was anymore, and now I'd started to see I could have everything I'd ever wanted without having to fight to preserve my name.

My father was a lot kinder since everything occurred, and we were bordering on a healthy father-son relationship that I never expected, but I was certainly glad it did. Though, when it came to the rest of my family, I was sure that everyone was a little apprehensive about Audrey getting so close to me, knowing that she was then going to write about all the things she experienced in our world. I fully supported her, though. I was never going to ask her to hide anything because I was glad she was telling the truth. It was going to bring about the kind of change that was needed in this socialite-rich community.

I grabbed a drink from the bar, sipping it slowly while I caught sight of Audrey smiling at me from the other corner of the room. I felt a light tap on my shoulder, and when I turned around to see the face that was standing behind me, I nearly dropped my drink.

"Hello, Jamie. It's been a long time."

"Charlotte," I said, feeling incredibly uneasy at the sight of her. "What are you doing here?"

"I think we need to have a talk."

She was the last person I ever thought I'd see again. Not now, not while I was finally getting to enjoy my life again. It had the work of Cece. After all, they were sisters, and I couldn't imagine she was happy that Eric left town after what happened.

It turned out, this was only the beginning.

Start reading book two "A Billionaire's Weakness" **here**.

CONNECT WITH THE AUTHOR

Join Ava Fox's Private VIP Reader Group here:

https://www.facebook.com/groups/573266000029256/

Facebook Page: https://www.facebook.com/AVA-

FOX-103067668333239

So if you liked this book, I`d like to ask for a small favor.Would
you be so kind to leave a review on amazon?
It would be very much appreciated!
The reason I'm asking for reviews: reader reviews are the lifeblood
of any author's career. For a humble typewriter-jockey like myself,
getting reviews (especially on Amazon) means I can submit my books for advertising. Which means I can actually sell a few copies
from time to time - which is always a nice bonus :)

Once again, thank you for your support - and enjoy
what's left of the weekend!

Printed in Great Britain
by Amazon